Other Books By Daniel Peterson

Short novels
Free Body Diagram
King of Shards

Novel
The Sunward Road

Comic strip book
reCYcled

NO WEEDS IN EDEN

by

Daniel Peterson

With editing assistance by Mary Foster.

First Edition (printed 2017)

Copyright © 2017 Daniel Peterson

Cover photos Copyright © 2017 Daniel Peterson

This book can be purchased, rated or reviewed at www.lulu.com .

ISBN: 978-0-9854957-9-4

NO WEEDS IN EDEN

1. Phia

Phia woke to the worst headache, ever, in her twenty-three years on this earth. Why? She had drunk two beers slumped in front of the television watching afternoon talk shows, then Junior came home, and then...what?

Phia lay still, eyes closed, swamped in pain, stretching for memory. She was chilled to the bone.

She felt around for bed covers, and realized that she lay not in bed but on hard floor. Phia opened her eyes. Pain flashed between her temples. It was night, the house was dark, but a streak of light from a streetlamp spilled through the window, just enough light to register that her vision was wonky. Rolling her face to the right gave view of the vertical bar of light falling on the front of the kitchen counter. The motion blasted new pain through her agony-filled head and yanked the hair behind her left ear as if somebody was standing on it. She was in the kitchen. She closed her eyes against the pain and her doubled view of the light stripe. Reaching her hand up and back, she delicately probed the sticky, crusted hair where blood had glued her to the floor.

A very bad cut lay under her fingers and the tug at her hair had broken the clot, releasing a fresh blood flow. Two beers would not split her head. What had?

Junior. Junior walked in the front door, high on meth or something, and blew up about her loafing around swilling beer at two in the afternoon. She flared right back, drank the last swallow in her beer can, threw it over her shoulder into the loose pile of dead cans in the corner, stood and strode into the kitchen with the raving Junior at her heels. She opened the refrigerator, pulled out a fresh beer, turned and...

That was as far as Phia's memory could take her. She remembered nothing from the moment of turning until the slow awakening on the kitchen floor.

But she could guess. No doubt Junior clocked her as soon as she turned. Yes, her nose and lips ached, and blood crusted her face. That bastard.

Where was the jackass now? It was dark; it had been hours since his fist slammed her head against the edge of the refrigerator. Then he must have run away, and wasn't that just like the chicken-shit asshole? Junior was a tough guy with her, but when the blood spurted, he would have been out the door like a rabbit.

It was not the first time that Junior hit Phia, but it would be the last, whether she died here on the linoleum, or because she gut-shot him the next time she saw him.

With that goal in mind she sat up unsteadily, ripping the rest of the clotted hair loose from the floor and immediately passing out again, only aware of the distant pop when her head smacked the linoleum. Thirty-five minutes later Phia re-awoke to reassemble the events which put her there in such pain. Again, she lifted her upper body off the floor, but slowly, her hands bracing against the floor to stop the swaying. Nausea welled up a small heave of nasty bile. It must have been even longer than she thought since the attack, for her stomach to be so empty. The foul goop crept down the inside of her thigh, darkening the worn denim. Phia didn't care, especially when she realized that she had also peed her pants. She coughed from the acid irritation in her throat and winced.

Fifteen hellish minutes later Phia was standing, leaning steeply forward with her quivering legs spread wide for stability and her hands gripping the edge of the counter. As the nausea faded, her thirst made her fumble with the faucet and a cup until she managed to drink. She hung her head, letting blood pressure build in her brain before she began side-stepping toward the back door, walking the counter edge with her hands.

A dilemma faced her at the door. Should she call 911 and wait for an ambulance, or should she continue outside to drive herself to the emergency room? Phia felt her pocket and found her phone. It was not broken, it was charged, and it flashed three-thirty-two in the morning. In the darkness her double vision was not obvious until the digital time glowed into her eyes. A different pocket produced the keys for her battered, old Geo Metro. She leaned her rump against the counter and weighed the keys against the phone on her palms.

If she left her car here, Junior would trash it before she got back. And she did not want to come back to collect it, at least not without a gun. Coming back would break the momentum she needed to get away from this life, a sudden revelation; she *had* to get away from this life. She would drive herself to the hospital, if she could get to the car. The broom, leaning by the door, would do as a walking stick.

Five wobbly minutes later, including a brief rest, the Geo's headlights lit the trash-filled back yard, looking twice as cluttered in her doubled vision. Phia experimented before backing into the alley, closing one eye and then the other, to determine which would be more trustworthy. The left worked marginally better.

The drive to the hospital was slow and harrowing, with several wrong turns as her brain trauma and one-eyed confusion hampered her driving. She parked far from other vehicles.

Phia took a two minute break to breathe, rest, bolster her strength and remember to remove the keys from the ignition.

She began the trip across the parking lot on foot but went through the emergency room door on hands and knees. The shame of urine soaked jeans didn't even occur to her. Phia happened to look up in the moment that the receptionist glanced toward the opening door, and she felt a brief pleasure at the widening of the lady's eyes as they lit upon the bloody devastation to Phia's face and head. That positive moment ended when she lost consciousness and her face skidded against the floor.

Dr. Genoa, inured to worse sights, did not cringe at Phia's black-and-blue mottled face and bandaged, partly shaved head. He *did* cringe at the prospect of what he must divulge to this young and, probably, attractive woman.

He asked Phia, "Can you call somebody to be with you?"

"No."

"There must be someone."

"I know a few people, but don't want Junior finding out where I am."

"Junior?"

"The guy who did this." She gestured at her face.

"Ah." The doctor frowned. "We have the pictures we took of your injuries when you checked in. You can press charges against this Junior person and put him where he belongs."

"Waste of time. He'd be out on bail in a day, lookin' to finish me off."

That disturbed Genoa. It was a side of life he heard

about, but never personally encountered.

"Doc," Phia said, "you been suckin' a lemon?"

He half-smiled. "Sorry. Med schools teach bedside manner now, but in my day..." He added some heart to his smile. Phia laughed lightly but briefly because it hurt too much.

"So?" Phia asked.

Genoa looked at his i-Pad. He checked the vital signs beeping from the video screen beside the head of his patient's bed. Everything he could do to avoid her eyes, he did. Phia cleared her throat.

Dr. G. finally engaged his patient's miss-aligned eyes and said, "You have a serious concussion. You're young, so if you get rest and therapy, you'll probably recover completely from that." He looked again at the i-Pad for a long time.

"But," Phia said.

He looked up. "But. Doctors hate that word. Start with the good news and lead into the bad." This time he looked out the window. "Pardon my dithering. So. The short and not-so-sweet." His focus swung back to her eyes. "Your cranial MRI revealed an aneurysm. Inoperable."

The doctor did not look elsewhere, now. He studied the swollen remains of Phia's face.

"Aneurysm?"

"Weakened artery. Ballooned out to a thin wall. Prone to rupture, stroke, and death in your case. It's a major vessel."

Phia's first emotion, and first expression, was relief. Well, she thought. It's all over. I can finally relax.

"Did Junior's punch make it?"

"No. It was probably a congenital flaw which expanded with age."

"How long do I have left?"

"I don't know. Six months, six years. But it could be a hopeful sign for your longevity that the blow to your head did not burst the aneurysm."

"I could go any time."

Hesitantly he said, "Yes."

"Then I better get outta here and find a good coffin."

"Not today," the doctor said. "You're in no shape to leave, and we have to monitor your brain for inflammation, swelling. If you look good tomorrow afternoon, you can probably go home."

"Not home. No more."

"But..."

"I lived on the streets before. I can do it again."

"No, you need a quiet home environment and somebody to watch you."

"Ain't gonna happen, Doc. And I can't even stay tonight. I only got $400 in the bank."

Genoa nodded; this type of need had been growing for a long time. "The social worker will come by your room later to explain payment plans and indigent fund qualifications. We'll work something out. But you can't leave today."

Phia shrugged and regretted it with the jolt of pain.

"All right?" the doctor asked

"Okay."

"Good. Now rest. Sleep if you can. If the pain becomes too bad to sleep, let the nurse know and we'll get you more medication."

Daniel Peterson

2. Junior

Tucker L. Bryant Jr. sat nervously in his car at the end of the alley which ran behind the house he rented. He flipped his internal conversation back and forth between telling himself to go find out, and cursing that damned bitch, Phia. He had valuable stuff in there, including a stash of product worth several thousand dollars. But maybe the cops were watching. And maybe her dead, fly-covered corpse was lying there beginning to stink up the place. He called her phone a couple of times, but she wasn't picking up, for whatever reason. From the end of the alley, he couldn't see past the neighbor's fence into the back yard to tell if her car was there. He'd better do a quick drive through, or a slow one. Maybe he should walk.

In the end he took a fast drive down the alley with a glance into the yard, proceeding straight on out the other end and away. Phia's car was gone. Twenty minutes later he came back, saw no suspicious activity, and parked in the back yard.

He walked in through the still open kitchen door, listening for alarming sounds. There was a low buzzing. Phia was not lying there by the fridge, but he almost puked when he saw the still-moist, clotted blood puddle. Yeah, there were flies.

Why the hell did she make him hit her? Every fucking thing he said went in one ear and out the other. Look at this place. Did she pick anything up? Did she clean? No, she watched talk shows and emptied beer cans down her bottomless gullet. Then she really went over the top, pulling that extra beer from the fridge to piss him off. Jesus, that made him crazy! But his meth-driven punch scared him. She bounced off the fridge, dropped like a sack of potatoes and didn't move. And the blood! It just kept pouring!

Hell with that; he had to take care of things.

Junior found his hidden product first; the thick envelopes were still taped to the back of the crisper drawers in the refrigerator. He took them out to the car and stuck them with duct tape to the back of the rear seats, beneath the fabric that lapped down at the top inside the trunk. There was a half kilo of unprocessed marijuana jammed behind the hot water tank in the basement that he stuffed under the spare tire. He pulled on a hooked wire that hung down in the drain pipe for the laundry, lifting out a double sealed baggie of meth. Then he carefully dismantled his hash oil still, wrapping the parts in his dirty laundry, and took those out. Finally, the butane canisters and his clothes. He would abandon the TV. He could buy another, better one after his next bulk sale.

Junior drove over to his friend Jolly's place. The grossly fat Jolly and his equally obese girlfriend, Doreen, lived in a trailer park with their two screaming boys, aged three and four. The kids drove Junior crazy, but it always made him laugh when they fought—which they did all the time—and called each other "s'it 'ead". "You s'it 'ead!" "No! You s'it 'ead." Eventually Doreen would scream, "Would you little shit heads shut up!" Jolly would turn to Junior and say, "Don't know where they get that shit." Hysterical.

Junior backed his car in beside the trailer and started unloading stuff from his trunk to carry across the back yard and store in the small, warped metal garden shed. As he shuttled the third load, butane canisters, across the trampled, dead grass, Doreen stepped out of the back door.

"Hey," she said. "You ain't puttin' that shit in there."

"Jolly said I could."

"Bullshit. Those things'll blow up in that hot shed and kill us all. I got kids here!"

"What'm I gonna do with 'em?"

"Shove 'em up yer ass, for all I care, but they're not goin' in the shed. And not in my house."

Junior glowered at her. If I was Jolly, he thought, I'd tune that fat bitch up. She has too much mouth on her. He looked around. "How about the freezer? Won't blow in the freezer."

Doreen thought about that. Other than a few pizzas and some hamburger, there was lots of room in the old freezer under the parking canopy. And Roger (aka Jolly) said Junior was paying three hundred bucks to sleep on the couch and store stuff till the end of the month.

She said, "You're not gonna run that still here."

"I'm lookin' for a place. And I'm product ahead. Don't worry."

She nodded. "Okay. The freezer." She turned and waddled back into the trailer.

Daniel Peterson

3. Phia

Phia's first response to the news of her impending death, that sense of relief and potential release, came in response to living an unkind life. She was born fatherless to a woman only interested in her own next pleasure, be it mind-addling drugs or the admiration of the newest man.

Seven year old Phia sits in the filthy couch watching television while her mother giggles in the bedroom with Carl, or Joe, or whatever this one's name is. Mom comes out, pink color in her cheeks, pulling her blouse shut and buttoning it. Carl is sending her to the liquor store. A while after Mom goes out, the hairy, disgustingly naked Carl slumps into the room and slouches on the couch beside Phia. He leans over her and insinuates a hand inside her pants. She stares fixedly at the television. It hurts. He fiddles with her and it hurts. She drops tears from her cheeks as she watches Itchy kill Scratchy again on the TV. Or is Scratchy killing Itchy? Carl's most nasty bit swells, but she refuses to see it. Which one is Itchy? Carl takes her hand and puts it on himself. Which is Scratchy? When Carl stops, he leans his stinky breath into her face and says, "If you tell anybody, I'll eviscerate your mom." Phia doesn't know what "eviscerate" is.

At nine years old, Child Protection removed her from her mother's custody to place Phia in a series of unsatisfactory foster homes.

Sixteen year old Phia abandoned foster care, as soon as she realized that the newest foster father was about to become her next abuser, and fearfully took up residence in urban crannies among a large population of similarly situated minors. These were the throw-aways, the kids booted from home for being gay or trans, or who ran from home to escape abuse, or who suffered mental problems which nobody cared to or tried to help.

She learned early that protection could be hired from a large male by providing frequent sex. Through care and luck she avoided boys and men who would have pimped her, rather than keeping her private. These relationships were roughly equivalent to assault by strangers, but at least she knew what to expect.

Phia traded protectors several times before reaching her majority, when she begged and stole enough money to improve her wardrobe at a thrift store and apply for a job waiting tables in a bar, a difficult process involving application for her birth certificate (including distasteful contact with her deteriorated mother), so she could apply for a social security card. Barmaid is what she was working at when she met the vicious Junior, and what she was still doing when she hobbled out of his back door, beaten and bloodied. It's why she had $400.

With assistance from the social worker, Phia applied for indigent status to pay the bills. To qualify, Phia said she was unemployed, which she was since she wouldn't be going back to the bar where Junior could find her. Doctor Genoa gave her prescriptions for hypertension and an anticoagulant, then dug in a drawer to pull out a double handful of each as free samples. He told the nurse to schedule Phia for a follow-up exam in three weeks. He waived his fee, then admonished her to find a comfortable place to live, and to not drive, never again. Driving would put others at risk. "And don't take any plane trips. A sudden drop in air pressure could trigger a rupture."

"Okay, Doc. Whatever you say. What do these meds do?"

"The first reduces blood pressure to ease stress on the aneurysm. The other is an anticoagulant. Aneurysms can develop zones of turbulent blood flow which promote clotting. If a clot breaks loose it can cause a stroke almost as serious as the aneurysm bursting."

He dug through a drawer. "Here," he said. "Read this pamphlet so you can recognize the signs of stroke. Call an ambulance immediately."

"Will it be the same if the aneurysm blows?"

The doctor hesitated. "Not likely. In that case you might feel or hear the tearing arterial wall, and then loss of consciousness in minutes or seconds."

"Thanks. Great. Now I know what to look forward to."

When she shuffled from the hospital the next day in clothes which a kind CNA had laundered for her, she went straight to her Geo Metro, climbed in, dropped the pills and prescription into the glove box, and drove away.

She spent two nights sleeping in her cramped car, eating apples, cheese, and crackers, drinking chocolate milk and gaining strength. Her eyes came back into alignment and her balance improved. On the second day a text message came from a casual friend at work, "Wher r u?" She did not respond. Later another text pinged in, "U OK?" Phia ignored that, too.

She drove by Junior's house on the third day. His car was gone so she parked around the corner, where she knew he never passed when returning home, and walked to the house. She passed through the kitchen, pausing to marvel at the size of the blood pool—dried now to a dark, hard crust. How did she survive that? She searched the rest of the house. Initially she thought that Junior might not have come back after attacking her and fleeing. But, that was wrong. He was there long enough to grab his clothes, dismantle his hash oil still and remove it along with the butane canisters. Phia's clothes and other personal items lay where she had left them, so she stuffed everything into plastic shopping bags and loaded the bags in the car. On the last walk to the Geo she glanced back at the house, longing for a quick shower, but stinking alive was better than stinking dead, so she kept going.

Phia took the one action still available to her: Running away—running from Junior, her mother, the dirty city, and doctors with bad news. She found the nearest on-ramp to I-80, pointing the car west, toward the setting sun.

The hospital gave Phia changes of bandage for seven days. That first evening on the road, she washed as well as possible in the restroom of the truck-stop where she planned to spend the night in her car. After peeling the day's bandage off, she gently soaped around the stitched injury, craning her neck and folding her ear forward to view the back corner of her head in the mirror. She rinsed off the soap with handfuls of water, patted the site dry with a paper towel, applied disinfectant to the wound and clumsily plastered on the new bandage.

Phia admired her greenish facial bruises, an improvement which assured her they would soon fade completely, but she shook her head in disgust at the large white bandage and patch of stubbly hair. When she left the restroom she paused at the hats display to pick out a bright orange, hunter's stocking cap. With it pulled far down over her ears, only the lowest corner of the bandage was visible, and the hairless surround barely noticeable. It was debatable whether this look was an improvement. Travel snacks joined the hat on the checkout counter.

As the clerk tallied up the cost, Phia said, "Wait." She walked over to the beer cooler and pulled out a six-pack of Guinness. "There," she said, placing it on the counter.

The next day, six hours and two fuel stops further down the road, Phia pulled into a remote rest area. The surrounding region was barren, dry and rocky. She strolled out into the rough land for a hundred meters with an open Guinness in her hand, sat on a rock with her back to the rest area and gazed out into wilderness. An urge tempted her to stand and keep right on walking, but she didn't. From the rest area her stocking cap was visible as a bright speck in gray-brown expanse, but none of the other pausing travelers noticed it. Forty-five minutes later, she still sat there and she was still alive.

I guess the time isn't right, she thought, then stood, turned and walked back to her Geo Metro.

There was no hurry, so she slept there that night, fading out to the strains of country music from a weak radio station.

Consistent with this dawdling pace, she didn't push the little, three cylinder Geo over fifty-five, and stopped to explore most of the small cities along the route; she had never been west of Omaha before.

Through the passing days the facial bruises vanished, the stubble hair grew longer, the bandage went by the wayside when supplies ran out, but the hat stayed to cover the angry looking scalp stitchery, still visible through the stubble. Bathing was a problem, as was clean laundry. She got some too-few showers at truck stops, but otherwise washed up a little at rest areas and fuel stations. Laundromats cost too much to justify the expense, so her underwear either got washed in bathroom sinks or in the shower with her. They couldn't be wrung completely dry so they spent most of the time laid out around the car interior. She didn't worry about washing the outerwear and lavished her armpits with deodorant. The jeans developed a shiny, brownish hue and shirtfronts acquired patterns of grease speckles from junk-food crumbs. Between rare changes, they lay among the underwear to air. Despite these attempts at cleanliness, she remained far from Godliness, developing a musty, sour odor that hung around her and inside the car.

Phia consumed the last of Dr. Genoa's free-sample meds, but she didn't bother finding a drug store to re-fill the prescription. She couldn't afford it and what would be the point?

4. Junior

Junior laid low at Jolly's, refusing to respond to texts and calls, watching the news for info about Phia, and asking Jolly every day if he'd heard anything. He was antsy to get out of there because trailer-trash Doreen had the nerve to treat *him* like *he* was dog shit, and the two little "s'it 'eads" drove him up the wall. To hurry his release, for twenty bucks and an offer to watch the "s'it 'eads", he talked Doreen into going to the bar where Phia worked and asking about her. It took Doreen so long, she must have spent the whole twenty bucks on booze before coming home. Nobody had heard from Phia, or seen her, or heard about her since the day before she fired up Junior's temper. So he came out of hiding, though he stayed away from the places where he would encounter Phia's friends.

First, he found another rental house. He moved in, set up manufacturing, and processed the last of his weed. Some clients wondered where he was and were comforted when he texted them and showed up again at his various points of sale.

Junior mostly supplied rc-sellers and the occasional suburbanite, so he didn't hang out on street corners. He selected several spots where highly mobile clients passed through continually, but anonymously and quickly, like convenience stores. He made sure he was not parked obtrusively, or he struck an arrangement with an employee, preferably a manager, so he would not be hustled off the property. The scheduled lengths of his meetings were brief, to reduce risk of attracting unwanted attention. In the back of his mind, he was planning to reduce his visibility by getting a couple more cars and rotating among them for deliveries.

Less than a month after the bitch Phia disrupted his life and cut his profits, he was back in business. The way he figured, she owed him for lost income, plus compensation for pain and suffering (living at Jolly's) and the inconvenience of having to relocate. If she was still alive, he planned to have a word or two with her.

5. Phia

During her exploration of Cheyenne, Phia noticed a little church and impulsively pulled into the parking lot. A reader board outside said, "Eternal life available here". That caught her attention—quickly approaching date with death and all. She walked to the door, stopping to touch the palm of her hand against it as if she could absorb that life right through the wood panel, then pulled it open. A desolation of hard, empty pews lay before her, much like the barren landscape at the rest area where she had walked into the wilderness and waited, willed, to die. She walked the echoing aisle to the middle of the room, sat to her right on the rock-like pew, and focused her eyes beyond the pulpit and beyond the wall behind it.

The minister walked in a half hour later. He spotted the compact young woman in the bright stocking cap and stopped with a frown. He went down the aisle to sit in the pew across from her, noticing the unwashed clothes, the musty scent, but smiled and said, "Can I help you?"

As if reality here suffered a time lag like a poorly synchronized movie, Phia paused for a time before retrieving her gaze and turning to the preacher. "No," she said. "Nobody can."

"My boss can."

Phia frowned in puzzlement, then smoothed her face. "Ah," she said, looking up at the cross behind the pulpit.

The minister nodded. He knew enough about mental health to recognize the flat emotional affect of post-traumatic stress syndrome. "But before we get into that, can I offer you a meal? A shower? Laundry?"

She focused. "That would be good." The guy looked trustworthy enough, but what did it matter? He couldn't do anything worse to her than she already faced. At least he was not overtly leching for her.

"What's your name?" he asked.

"Phia."

"Short for Sofia?"

"Just Phia."

"I'm Richard." He stood, gesturing her to follow.

They left the pews, went out the side entry and she was still not dead. They walked next door to the preacher's home, where he introduced Phia to his wife, Ruth, a tall muscular woman in her forties. Shaking Phia's hand, as the odor wafted up, Ruth said, "Oh, my!"

"Sorry," Phia said. "Been on the road a long time."

"That's okay. We'll have supper in an hour. Why don't you get a bath, or shower. But bring all your clothes in first so I can get them started in the washer."

Phia nodded and left the house, returning with a loose, smelly stack of clothes. Ruth held out a basket into which Phia dropped the load.

"Now," Ruth said, "go get that bath, but toss out your clothes when you're undressed. When you finish you can use my bathrobe, hanging on the inside of the door. Here, give me the hat."

Reluctantly, Phia pulled it off and handed it to Ruth.

Ruth maintained a neutral expression while she said, "I'm pretty good with shears. After supper I could trim that hairdo into something more flattering."

"Okay."

Richard was good to his word, and did not bring up his Boss during supper. They confined conversation to small-talk which did not address Phia's state. He saw that Phia was struggling to keep her eyes open during dessert, so he suggested that Ruth make up the guest bed while he put away the leftovers, scraped the dishes and loaded the dishwasher. Tomorrow was another day with another opportunity, he thought, unaware of Phia's curtailed potential tomorrows.

Phia woke up disoriented. It was the first time in four weeks that she had not slept in the Geo, so she lay immobile until she remembered the church, Richard and Ruth. She looked around. Her clean and folded clothes lay on a cedar chest under the window. She yawned. It was time to get back on the road.

At the breakfast where they insisted she join them, Richard asked, "Why?"

"Why what?"

"Why do you *have* to get back on the road?"

She thought about this now for the first time since driving onto I-80. Then, it was just about finally waking up to the perpetual misery of her life, a suddenly shortened life, wanting to get away from Junior and the town where he and all the misery existed, and seeking absorption in the motion of the car and the hazy destination, so she didn't have to think or feel.

"I just... I just have to see stuff. I have to do stuff."

And sitting in this calm house, without the rhythms of the car, she realized the truth of this. If anybody needed to complete a bucket list, it was she. But she'd better hurry. And she had to make a list first.

Ruth said, "You're young. Young people do that. But aren't you lonely?"

"Lonely is where I've always lived."

After an uncomfortable pause, Richard said, "You should stay awhile in Cheyenne. There's a place supported, in part, by our church where you could live, rest, assess your situation, and decide how to proceed. Counseling is available there for free."

"You know," Phia said slowly, "I'm an atheist. I only stopped at your church because I like your sign. You're nice people, and I appreciate your help, but you don't have anything for me. There's no God in my life. The Devil, sure. No God. I'll take off now." She stood up.

Richard said, "We might be able to help. It's worth a try."

She shook her head and walked toward the bedroom to collect her clothes.

"Wait," Ruth said, shoving back her chair. "Let's get you that hair cut."

Phia stopped. She turned. "Thanks. I'd like that."

When Ruth started, she had to restrain a gasp at sight of the long, fresh, barely hidden scar. Phia's growing-out hair was just long enough to be influenced by a comb, but asymmetrical haircuts were in fashion so Ruth trimmed to that same length, straight from the top of the short patch, forward above the left ear to Phia's temple. With the rest shaped but left longer, the look was not too bad. In fact, because Phia's face was mildly asymmetrical itself (she had one eye slightly higher and larger, and a lopsided, if rare, smile) the unbalanced haircut countered it, somewhat. Phia looked in the mirror, content, thanked Ruth, and later packed the orange hat in with her clean clothes.

When Ruth and Richard still could not convince her to stay, they gave her an old duffle bag to carry her clothes and a cheap cooler loaded with semi-perishable foods.

The preacher and his wife waved to Phia as she drove out of the church parking lot, but she was already focused on her road to the setting sun, and didn't see them.

Phia worked on her bucket list. Some obvious choices for a young woman of reduced expectation were automatically eliminated: A husband, children, a college education, a career. What next? Genuine love? That was pure fantasy in her experience. Let's lower the bar, she thought. Nice scenery. Okay. That's doable and I've seen some already. Meet more nice people. Climb a mountain, or not, considering the aneurysm. Learn to ski. Go sailing. Fly a plane—no, the doc said no planes. Learn to play a musical instrument (probably not enough time for that, at least not enough to be any good). Paint a picture. Make a viral on-line video. Audition for a play. Sing in a chorus.

She pulled out her phone at the next rest stop to log into her bank account. The balance would not take her much further before she would have to find an income, or there would be no point in making her list.

Leisurely days beyond Cheyenne, after her exploration of Salt Lake City, a whim turned Phia north onto I-15, toward

Idaho, the state that everybody confused with Iowa. She knew Iowa, but what was Idaho besides potatoes and neo-Nazis?

The exit sign for I-84 mentioned Boise, the only Idaho town name she recognized, so she held that lane. The day's drive extended beyond her usual because the only rest area along the route felt too creepy to stay there over night. Finally, she pulled off the freeway at an Idaho town called Burley, found a Walmart not far from the freeway, parked in a far corner of the lot and, after a visit to the store restroom, bedded down in her car.

So far, what she found in Idaho looked much like what she had seen in Nebraska, Wyoming and Utah—lots and lots of very little.

Phia washed in the Walmart restroom the next morning, then replenished her food supply in the grocery section. A potbellied man in front of her, only slightly taller than her five feet three, wearing camo, twenty years older than she, and carrying a toddler through the checkout line, leered suggestively at her, so she figured that the damage Junior had made didn't show anymore. Or maybe it wouldn't matter to this jerk. He obviously didn't mind the renewed patina of travel soil clinging to her.

"Nice morning," he said to Phia.

She ignored him with her oblique, dazed look.

He frowned, shrugged and checked out.

After paying, Phia waited just inside the store exit, watching the creep until he put the kid in a child seat and left, then she went out and made breakfast in her car.

Phia ate, watching the occasional early-hour cars enter and leave the lot, jolted by recognizing among them the creep from checkout driving slowly through without the kid, looking around but not seeing her and not parking. She relaxed.

She was tidying up after her meal when she heard a sound and looked up to see a car parked nose-to-nose with hers. She sighed at the inevitability; it was the creep. Phia locked her door and started the engine. Camo-creep was approaching her driver's side window with his version of a charming smile, which made her shudder.

Did she have some kind of "victim" stamp on her forehead, which only she couldn't see? What was it about her that lured predators? She backed the car away as he gestured for her to roll down her window. She steered to clear him and his car, then started forward but he stepped in front of her. Phia shook her head and stopped. He put his hands out in a pleading gesture. Phia looked around the lot for help or witnesses and the creep did too, smiling broader at the lack of people. She flipped him the finger. He lost the smile and signed for her to turn off the engine. Phia started forward again, turning further, and Creep moved over in front again. When she stopped, the Geo was almost against his knees. She gestured for him to move aside, but he shook his head, signing again to shut off the ignition. Phia shrugged and started slowly forward, pushing against his legs so he had to back up. He slammed his palm on her hood and she flinched but kept pushing, just a little faster. Soon he was scrambling backward with his hands pressed against the hood so she continued to accelerate until he jumped aside. As she passed him, he swung his fist at her window but hit the door post, yelped, and failed to remove his left foot from the path of the rear tire. As she sped out of the lot she looked in the mirror to see him sitting on the pavement, untying his shoelace with the left hand while he sucked on the knuckles of the right.

Phia checked the gas gauge. It was getting low, but she did not want to fuel up in Burley and give the creep time to inspect his foot, climb into his car and go looking for her. His type, which she knew much too well, would rocket into a rage at not only being thwarted but also hurt by his intended victim. She drove north to the ramp and returned to the freeway, rolling west.

Violin, she thought. If she wanted to learn to play music, at least that was portable. Piano would be impractical. But violins don't even have frets; how can anybody figure out where their fingers go? Maybe a guitar. She looked around the cluttered, stuffed interior of her tiny car. Maybe an ukulele. In any case, she would need a job, as soon as her mindless, fleeing phase was finished. If she lived that long.

That afternoon she was exploring Boise, which she deemed a confusing maze, when she came upon the Morris Hill cemetery. She stopped to admire it and decided to picnic there.

A large, sixty-ish, overweight woman with a camera and a cane hobbled by taking photos of gravestones while Phia prepared food. The woman looked at her, spoke a greeting, then walked up and said, "You've chosen a nice place for a picnic. I sometimes come here just for the peace. Are you a Boise resident?"

"No," Phia said. "Just passing through. You want a sandwich?"

"No, thank you. Where are you from?"

"Iowa. Chocolate milk?"

"No, thanks. I have friends in Iowa."

Phia nodded. She wished that she, herself, did. While Phia ate, the woman stood balancing with her cane, visiting. The woman spoke like a college professor, explaining her self-imposed job collecting pictures of headstones to post on the internet.

"And it gets me out of the house," the woman said. "To where are you traveling?"

"The setting sun."

"Just a direction? No destination?"

"No. Just rolling."

"What will you do when you reach the ocean?"

"Don't know."

"Well, I wish you good roads. I must get on with my work. It has been a pleasure speaking with you."

Phia gave a little wave of the hand. The large lady smiled and shambled away between the graves.

Well, Phia thought, I can put one check mark beside the "meet more nice people" item on my list.

The early September day was sunny without being hot. She felt comfortable here. She felt calm. This spot, the nice picnic and the friendly woman washed away the bad taste left by her morning adventure in the Walmart parking lot. Still looming above all of this was the fact that she was in no better a position than the day she started west—worse, in fact, considering that her resources were now seriously diminished and her accelerated clock had ticked through several weeks; even in dog years, her remaining time wouldn't bring her to three score and ten. Checking her bank account she discovered that she would soon be at the end of her trip. If she had ever, in her disappointed life, been allowed any hope, she would have started looking for work here in Boise before her money ran out. Instead, she loaded back into the car and aimed south to the freeway.

Forty-five minutes down the road, eye-weary from the sun glaring through her windshield, Phia pulled into a truck stop that featured a motel and steady traffic. She felt secure here and, given the barrenness of the landscape, she didn't expect a suitable overnight stop further along.

The bathroom was deplorable, but better than washing from a pan or going without. She swapped underwear and laundered her worn set in the sink.

The early night was restless, with late arriving cars flashing headlights through her windows and diesel trucks idling a short distance away. Near midnight, she slept.

The next morning, awakened by a full bladder, and envying how men can pee into a bottle, she saw the most beautiful man she had ever seen walk from the motel to the convenience store.

Probably just another asshole, she thought. In fact, with looks like that, more likely an asshole.

She watched him walk back five minutes later. "My god," she muttered, then he turned and saw her looking through the side window of her car, and he smiled at her. Phia blushed. She looked away.

"He's an asshole," she said, "or he wouldn't smile at me and my 'victim' stamp."

Phia was ready to leave after a visit to the toilet and a small breakfast. Just before she started her car, she saw the beautiful man leave his room to stash bags in the trunk of a small, expensive car. Another beautiful man came from the same room, joining the first in the car. It sped away.

She shrugged.

Cranking up the Geo's engine, she resumed her trip. Phia realized that soon she would be leaving Idaho for Oregon even though it seemed she had seen very little of Idaho—an unsatisfactory little of Idaho. The map showed that the larger dimension of the state, if less area, lay toward Canada. Almost at the Oregon border, the exit for Hwy 95 appeared and she submitted a second time to her whimsy to turn north.

Phia's day ended at a scenic rest area on the Little Salmon River. The lack of cell phone connection was distressing, but it was pretty and refreshing after the desiccated drive across I-84. Finally she was seeing a part of the state which varied from dull expanse, though driving some of the scenic portions and their winding roads—uncomfortably near to steep, rock-bound, frothing streams, tailed too closely by giant, impatient trucks—nearly scared the pee out of her. It was not like driving in the flat-lands.

Daniel Peterson

6. Phia, Aaron and Nick

Phia topped off her gas tank in Lewiston, but gave up the idea of staying the night there, or even of exploring the town after she was overwhelmed by the stink of the giant paper mill across the river. She checked her account balance, just enough left for another stock of groceries, or another quarter tank of gas, or a few beers in a quiet bar. Beer felt irresistible. Her trip was almost over.

She cruised slowly into Moscow, a clean, agriculturally centered, university town. The rolling, wheat-stubble covered hills in which it lay were both lovely and unique—soft, curved, sensual mounds, too steep to imagine how they could be farmed. Two passes through the town center, and a sudden desire to stop, left her parked behind a bar and pizza hall called The Fleidermaus, installed in a former church. Its most potent mixed beverage was called The Belfry.

Looking around inside The Fleidermaus she had an epiphany, that bars are bars, and people in bars are people in bars, whether in Iowa, or Idaho, or anywhere else in the world.

She mounted a stool at the bar and ordered a Black Butte Porter. The bartender asked for identification, which she presented. She worked in a place much like this, and the sights, smells and noise of it felt comforting.

The bartender passed again so she called to him, "You need another server? I'm looking for work. Have experience."

"Sorry," he said. "Not hiring."

She shrugged. She sipped beer. It's not like she

expected any different. Looking at the servers working the tables, she guessed that university students filled all the positions, and, given the time of year, the fall term must have just started; plenty of meat to choose from. Phia leaned her back against the bar to watch the sparse crowd and settled into the challenge of stretching her last dollars as far as they could go.

At the fourth order, the bartender told her that her debit card was rejected.

"Wait," she said, checking every slot in her wallet, then digging in her jeans pocket for change. She closed the wallet, shrugged, put it back in her pocket, and looked at him piteously. He pulled the glass full of lovely, dark fluid back off the bar and poured it down the drain. Phia almost wept—what a shameful waste of good beer. In her time behind the bar, she let the patron have the drink and paid out of her own pocket, both to save wasting it, and because anybody who just spent their last dollar really needed a beer.

Phia needed more. She wanted to get drunk, but had only reached relaxation. Looking over the sparsely populated tables she spotted two round-faced, ordinary men in overalls visiting over a mostly eaten pizza and a partial pitcher of beer. The bartender turned his back to Phia, so she snatched an empty, used glass off the bar and wove her way over to the two men. She sat in an open chair.

"Hi, guys. You have room for one more?"

Aaron and his younger brother Nick looked at her with a mixture of alarm and curiosity. They saw a short, shapely woman with close, brown hair, and a pretty but lopsided face which gave her an expectant or questioning look. They glanced at each other and shrugged.

"Sure. I'm Aaron, this is my brother Nick."

She studied them. Aaron appeared late twenties, Nick much younger, near her own age.

"I'm Phia," she said, pushing her empty glass across the table.

Nick lifted the pitcher and drained it into her glass.

"Are you having more?" Phia asked, raising her glass.

Aaron turned to wave a server over to their table. "Another pitcher, please," he said. "Want some pizza, uh, Phia?" He pushed the pan toward her a quarter inch, since it already sat under her chin.

"Sure." She sipped her beer and made a little face. "Lager," she said.

Nick said. "Simple tastes. Lager beer and pepperoni pizza."

"No, no. I like them both. I just prefer that Black Butte Porter they sell here." She picked a slice of pizza. She bit off the point and asked while chewing, "You guys come here a lot?"

"Is that a pickup line?" Nick asked, smiling.

The beer had definitely relaxed Phia. She forgot her date with death, and forgot her poor luck with men.

"Don't know yet."

The men both drank the last of their beers. They watched her eat and wash the pizza down with gulps from her glass.

Aaron said, "We don't come here a lot, but tonight we're celebrating."

"Congratulations. Celebrating what?" She raised her

glass to them, drained it and bit again into pizza. She looked around for the server with the next pitcher.

"Big step in house remodel. You from around here?" Nick asked.

"No. From a galaxy far, far away—the Midwest. Me and Toto just dropped into Bumluck, Idaho out of a tornado."

The pitcher arrived. Aaron topped off Phia's glass and poured a half glass each for himself and Nick.

"You not drinkin'?" Phia asked.

"We have work in the morning," Nick said.

"Thank god somebody does," she said.

As she drained the pitcher alone, her conversation became more wild with each glassful. Near the bottom she blurted, "Just thought of a new entry for m' list. Sex wi' two men at once. Whatcha say? You're a couple o' nice guys. Wanna help me wi' m' list?"

Nick pulled Phia's car up to the garage door. He shut off the engine, climbed out and locked the car. The pushy young woman had become incoherent—comatose with open eyes. They discussed what they should do with her. They couldn't leave Phia on her own and Nick couldn't take a stray, drunk woman home to the apartment he shared with his girlfriend Patty.

Nick said, "You're gonna have to take her, Aaron."

"And put her where?"

Nick glanced at her. "I doubt she'll care."

She was happy to leave with them but incapable of

pointing out which car was hers. Finally Nick stuck his hand in her pocket to find her keys.

"Hey! Tha' tickles," she protested.

In the light from the streetlamp, Nick looked at the keys, noting the GM logo on one. He looked around the lot until he spotted the Geo Metro and walked over to it. Iowa plates. The key opened the door.

"No room for her in here," he called to Aaron when he saw the heap on the passenger seat and the packed rear. "We'll have to put her in your truck."

"Toto there?"

"No dog. But smells like one died in here." He cranked the window down.

She was just aware enough to sit upright in the truck and get buckled in place.

"I'll follow you," Aaron said.

Nick and Aaron slid the rag-doll Phia out of Aaron's truck cab and braced her upon wobbly legs. They walked her to the house and held her upright while Aaron juggled his keys one-handed to unlock the front door. Inside, they worked her through the cluttered living room which functioned for the moment as their woodworking shop, then down the hall and into the bedroom.

"Hold it," Aaron said, flipping the covers back from the near bedside. They laid her upper body down on the sheet with her legs dangling over the side of the queen bed.

"Uhh..." she said.

"Can you handle it from here?" Nick asked.

"She doesn't look too dangerous. I think I'll be okay."

"Then good luck. See you tomorrow."

Nick left Aaron to his chore.

Working with dim light bouncing in from the living room, Aaron lifted each of Phia's feet in turn, opening the Velcro straps of her shoes, pulling them off and stripping the short socks. The smell pushed him back. He set them out in the hallway. He turned to the task of unbuttoning and unzipping her jeans, then carefully lifted her rump off the bed to start them down her hips.

Another fuzzy moan eked from her.

Bending and grabbing her cuffs, he lifted her legs and tugged the jeans down, stopping briefly to pull her descending panties back up, gently lowering her feet before they cleared the jeans waistband. He threw the jeans into the hall with the shoes and socks.

The shirt would have been a challenge if it was a tight pullover, but it was a baggy button-front. He unbuttoned it, pulled her loosely upright and stripped it off. It flew out the door.

Once she was down to underwear, and he bent to raise her legs and turn her body onto the bed, he noticed that most of the smell had accompanied the outer clothing. He rolled her on her side toward the edge of the bed in case she vomited, pulled the light covers over her and set an empty joint-compound bucket on the floor below her face.

Aaron collected the soiled pile from the hallway. He took it to the basement, dumped everything, including the shoes, into the washing machine, slopped in soap, and pressed start. He doubted that Phia would worry about washing unsorted clothes.

Back upstairs, Aaron stepped into the makeshift kitchen (other bedroom) to prime the coffee pot and set its timer for the morning. He shut off the living room light, paused to let his eyes adjust, returned to the dark bedroom, stripped down to his briefs, and settled into bed far from Phia. If there was another bed, or even a couch, they would have separate accommodation, but he was not going to sleep on that hard floor, even for the modesty of this woman. Considering some of the drunken remarks she made earlier, she shouldn't mind.

Phia awoke with the second worst headache she could remember, chilled by the fear that she was still lying bloody and battered on Junior's kitchen floor. Hazy memories of the previous evening surfaced and she relaxed. She was not in Des Moines. She was in Bumluck, Idaho.

She lay on her side. It was dark, with a lighter square that must be a curtained window. She stroked her hand over the sheet and mattress. She had to pee really bad. Her senses sharpened until she heard the sonorous breath of a person sleeping behind her.

Oh, god, she thought. I've done it again.

This was how she met Junior, and the disgusting Benjy before that. Benjy was another real sweetheart. He coerced her into performing very personal acts upon herself while he recorded video. Then he uploaded the video to some web site to become a public embarrassment, available to all, forever. She complained and he said they would make a bundle of money, but she never saw a penny. Not long after that, Phia met Junior, got drunk with him, slept with him, moved in with him, and never saw the jerk Benjy again.

Phia lifted her knee to open her thighs, reaching down between her legs. She was wearing her panties, and there was no excess dampness, or slipperiness, or dried, crusty proteins. Nor was there a wet spot under her. There had been no sex. And her brassiere was still in place. But she had to pee.

Still half drunk, she raised the covers to twist out of bed, stood unsteadily, then staggered toward the lighter rectangle of the open door, glancing once at the figure under the bed-cover. When she reached the door, a voice came from the bed. "You okay?"

"Need the toilet."

"Turn right, first door on your right."

Phia braced on the doorjamb as she passed through, saw the dim, puzzling, unidentifiable clutter of the "kitchen" across the way. She ran her hand along the wall for balance. She looked out into the living room at the dark jumble and the exposed windows. Oh, Christ, she thought, no curtains. Why do I get all the losers? She turned into the bathroom.

Aaron heard the door close, noted that she did not bother to lock it, saw light flash from under it to reflect off the far hallway wall. The toilet seat came down a bit hard, then brief silence before he heard urine cutting into water. He thought this should not give him an erection, but it did. He was missing his estranged wife, Stephanie. A muffled rattle, silence, then the toilet flushed. In a moment, water ran in the sink. Aaron waited for the door to open, but it didn't.

"Do you have Tylenol?" Phia called.

"Aspirin. In that rack on the right end of the counter. Right in front."

"Mind if I use your cup?"

"Hold on. You don't want to use that dirty thing."

He rolled out of bed, grabbed his overalls and pulled

them on, tucking himself in discretely. He went across the hall to the "kitchen". Phia heard the clink of porcelain, the crinkling of food packaging, a silence, and he came across the hall. She had opened the door, where she stood waiting with three tablets in her hand.

"Here," Aaron said, holding out two soda crackers spread with butter. "Eat these first. That aspirin will tear your gut up."

There had been little light when he undressed her, so now his eyes glanced down impulsively over her bra, panties, legs, then pausing again at each point of interest on the way back up. The compact, young woman carried a pleasing set of shapes. Thank goodness for his confining overalls. She watched the track of his eyes without surprise or expression.

"Are you gay?" she asked.

Aaron chuckled. "No," he said.

She looked down at the lump in his overalls. "No, I guess not."

"Why do you ask?" he asked.

"I just never slept with a man who didn't touch me," she said as she took the crackers and cup from his hands.

"You passed out. It would have been against the law, and rude."

She cocked her head. "Never stopped any guy before."

Phia chewed on crackers, ran water in the cup, washed them down, popped in the tablets and then more water. And then two more cups of water.

She set the cup down on the counter. "You're a funny guy," she said.

He moved to let her pass out of the bathroom and over to the bedroom, running his gaze down and up her body again from behind, then, as she sat on the edge of the bed, he turned off the bathroom light. He felt his way through the door to his side of the bed, dropped his overalls and crawled under the covers, adjusting his erection to a more comfortable angle before settling.

"By the way," he said. "I threw your clothes in the washing machine. I'll put them in the dryer when I get up. You sleep until you feel better."

"If you weren't going to touch me, why are we in the same bed?"

"It's the only bed in the house, I didn't want to sleep on the floor, and I can't make a guest sleep on the floor either."

"If I was a man, would you still do that?"

He considered. "No," he admitted. "You'd be in your car, behind the bar."

"Well, you're honest, but you're still a funny guy," she said, and rolled away from him to wait for the aspirin to take effect.

Phia woke to a full bladder again and sounds of footsteps and clunking objects in the bathroom. Coffee smell wafted from the room across the hall, and her head hurt again. She swung out of bed dizzily, stood and looked around the room. A couple of work shirts lay on the dresser in the corner, so she stepped over to them and put one on, buttoning it as she shuffled toward the door.

Rounding the corner of the bathroom doorway she stopped, surprised at the change since the night before.

Aaron said. "Let me get out of here so you can use it." He moved into the hall and Phia stepped into the bathroom. "Nice shirt," Aaron said.

She looked at him blankly, closed the door and used the toilet. She noted that what's-his-name (Adam?) was clearing out everything, including the large mirror that had been hanging on the wall. The outline of it still showed. Her cup and the aspirin were gone, as well as the soap, but she rinsed her hands, drying them on the tails of the over-sized shirt.

The man was sitting in the living room with one thigh on a sawhorse, sipping coffee. The darkened living room clutter remembered from her hazy walkabout in the wee hours was now revealed in sunlight to be woodworking tools and supplies.

"How you doing this morning?" Aaron asked with a knowing smile.

Phia grimaced. "Still breathing, but I'd be better if you could please tell me were you put the aspirin."

"In the kitchen. Not the makeshift one, the real one. Around that corner." He nodded.

She followed the nod around the corner and stopped. The kitchen contrasted with the rest of the house—sparkling, fresh and beautiful. "Nice," she said.

"That's what we were celebrating last night. Finishing the kitchen."

"It's gorgeous."

"Thanks. Find the aspirin?"

"Yeah, thanks." She rattled three out of the bottle, filled the cup at the faucet and threw the tablets into the back of her mouth.

She returned to the living room. Her mind put the puzzle together. The lack of curtains was not bachelor fundamentals, it was the remodel. And with the kitchen finished, Adam was starting to dismantle the bathroom.

"Mind if I get a quick shower before you tear out the tub?"

"Get it while you can. After today we'll be using the shower stall in the basement, and it has spiders."

She shuddered. "Thanks. You have towels?"

"In my dresser. Bottom drawer."

After the shower, she dried off, put on just the shirt, without her dirty underwear, and came out. "I needed that. Thanks for waiting. It's all yours."

Aaron carried his coffee with him to the bathroom.

Phia investigated the main floor, hunting for the laundry, then traipsed down the basement steps. She pulled her clean clothes out of the dryer and dressed without underwear. She would wash all of her clothes, then she'd have clean to put on. She had not considered that this guy might boot her out as soon as she was dressed. She studied the controls on the washer and dryer.

Upstairs, she looked out the front window at her car in the driveway. She had not driven and parked there, or it would have new dents. Phia went into the bedroom and looked on Aaron's nightstand and dresser for her keys, but did not find them. She stood outside the bathroom door asking, "Do you know where my car keys are?"

"On the windowsill by the front door."

"Cool."

She snapped up her keys on the way out, gathered her filthy laundry and came back with it stacked in her arms, proceeding straight to the basement.

Two minutes later, with the washing machine sloshing behind her, she returned to the main floor.

"Is there coffee left?"

"Yeah. In the back room. We aren't in the real kitchen yet."

She fetched her cup and went to fill it.

"You need cream or sugar?" Aaron called.

"No. I take it black."

"I figured. Like your beer."

She leaned against the bathroom doorjamb to watch Aaron/Adam. Phia recalled differences that she noticed between the two brothers last night. This one was a little bigger, had a deeper voice, and laughed less readily.

He said, "You hungry?"

"Ooopff. No. Not yet."

Aaron was detaching fixtures in preparation for removing the sink. He managed the drain and hot water supply tube, but was struggling to release the cold water. Aaron was six feet tall, no body builder but well muscled from an active life. He could reach his arms into the tight cabinet under the sink, or his head and shoulders, but not everything. He couldn't see what he was doing and his large hand barely fit between the cabinet partition and the water connection. He tried by hand, then with Channel-Locks, but kept missing the connector, or slipping and bashing sharp objects.

"Damn!"

He pulled his hand out and looked at the bloody knuckles.

"Can I help?" Phia asked.

Aaron scowled dubiously, then shrugged. "Sure, give it a try."

She gestured for the headlamp Aaron was wearing. She lay on her back on the floor and scootched her way into the small cabinet until she could look up behind the sink. Ignoring her throbbing head, she reached up with the Channel-Locks, gripped the stubborn coupling and, little-by-little in the cramped slot, backed it off. Water dribbled on her face, making her sputter.

Aaron watched her shirt ride up as she stretched her arms overhead, exposing her midriff with the belly flattened by the curving of her back over the lip of the cabinet base. It was a nice belly. The stretching slimmed it, accentuating the feminine, hourglass shape from hips to breasts. He saw that her breasts must be unrestrained to rest as they did under the shirt.

"Got it."

"Before you come back out, can you unhook the drain stopper lever?"

"I'll try."

She fiddled with that for a while, then handed out some parts. "Here."

"One more thing. Can you loosen the retainers around the sink?" He sipped his coffee. Aaron was enjoying the entertaining break.

"What retainers?"

"You'll need this screwdriver." She took it from his hand. "Now, look right up to the cabinet top around the sink. You'll see some screw heads on small, funny shaped parts."

"Funny shaped?"

"Kind of like an 'L'."

She grunted. "Tough, but they're coming."

"When they're loose they can be turned so they don't hook under the counter top, and we can pull the sink."

In a couple of minutes she lowered her arms and looked out at Aaron's legs. "That's hard on the arms and neck. Anything else while I'm here?"

"That's it, come on out."

She hunched out of the cabinet, her shirt riding up tantalizingly higher, and he gave her a hand up.

"Thanks," Aaron said. "That's a big help."

"Being small has a few advantages."

Phia stepped back outside the bathroom door, taking her coffee cup with her. She watched him work a putty knife around the sink to break the caulking loose.

Aaron asked as he worked, "So what's your deal?"

"What do you mean?"

"Last night you latched onto me and Nick like a drowning woman. What's the story?"

She shrugged. "Nothing. I just wanted to get drunk. My money's gone. You were handy."

"And we're only men, and you're good looking, and how the hell could we refuse?"

"Good looking, Adam?"

"Like you don't know. And it's Aaron. That was the whole plan? Get drunk?"

"For last night, yeah."

"And today?"

She studied him. "Find a place to park the car where I won't get rousted by the cops for living in it, and start looking for work."

"Mighty small car."

"Not my favorite motel, but it works." She looked around. "Though I'd rather be inside."

"You asking to stay here?"

"Not free. I paid for a lot of stuff with the only thing I have." She set her cup down, stuck her index fingers in her jeans pockets and thrust her pelvis twice. "I'm out of money, but I'll pay what it takes until I get a job. Can you put me up till I find something? I'll make it right."

Aaron looked askance at her, but didn't speak.

She asked, "You married? Not that it matters."

"Barely. Soon not. And you're right, it doesn't matter." He paused, evaluating her hopeful expression. "I'll talk to Nick, but I think we can let you stay for a while without..." He glanced at her pelvis. "Anyway, given the job you just did under that sink, we can probably use you outside of a bed."

Phia said, "Cool."

Aaron called on Nick's lunch break and talked over the issue of Phia. Nick was okay with it and swung by his apartment after work to pick up a cot, camping pad, and two sets of twin sheets. For some reason, as he drove, a tune from *The Sound of Music* kept cycling through his brain until he could put words to it: "How do you solve a problem like our Phia?"

Daniel Peterson

7. Phia and Steph

Phia was in the bathroom putting the second coat of mud on the new gypsum board. The mud wouldn't lie flat for her, but Aaron said it wasn't critical up to the third coat, and she needed the practice. She still overworked the mud, trying to make it smoother, and dragging the trowel across already drying portions gave her fits.

A week before, the Giffin brothers set her up with the cot and a yard-sale dresser in the unfinished basement bedroom. When they had moved the dresser in, the boys looked skeptically at the window high up on the wall.

Aaron asked, "You think you could climb through that in case of a fire?"

"Sure, if the dresser's there."

"Show us," Aaron said, dragging the dresser across the floor to the window.

Phia climbed up, stood there on her knees at the window and tried to open it. "It's stuck."

Nick tried the window and said, "Hold on." He left the room, returning with a screwdriver and a plastic bottle of graphite powder. Nick pried at the sliding window with the screwdriver, squirting powder in every joint. Then he applied enough muscle to make it slide, and ran it back and forth until it eased.

"Now try."

Phia climbed back on the dresser and slid the window.

She stuck her arms out, and head and chest, put the right foot up on the dresser beside her left knee, pushing herself up and through until her hips encountered the frame. She stopped then to wriggle a little, shoved with her feet and inched through while the dresser toppled to be caught behind her by the Giffins. Without solid footing it took almost a minute for her to worm completely out.

Aaron and Nick looked at each other.

Aaron said, "We'll screw the dresser to the studs."

"We can put some handles on the outside wall above the window that she can grab. She has to go out on her back."

Aaron called through the window, "We have some ideas. Come around and we'll try again."

"Too far," she shouted. "Catch me." Then she lunged back through the window as the brothers jumped around the dresser to support her—an impromptu trust-exercise from some confidence building seminar—and pulled her the rest of the way. They cradled her, trying to avoid too intimate contact, and stood her on the floor.

They fixed the escape route. She moved her clothes from the duffle bag, that Richard and Ruth had given her, into the worn dresser. Living in the basement gave her a special comfort; she was close to the working bathroom. Aaron had to climb the stairs. The one downside was the highly mobile population of big, hairy wolf spiders.

Nick showed up after his job every day and the three of them labored together, Phia contributing whatever unskilled effort she could. While they worked, Phia learned about Aaron's wife, Stephanie, blowing up over this very house when Aaron quit his job fighting wildfires and went into the partnership with Nick fixing and reselling homes. The final straw for Stephanie was when the company she worked for folded and her job vanished. She stormed out on Aaron in a panicked rage. Now she was looking for work, living on unemployment insurance and their savings. Aaron also had to tap the savings to live and buy remodel supplies, so it was dwindling quickly. Aaron mentioned rumors that Steph had begun consoling herself with alcohol. She sounded like a real prize. Phia did not take into account the natural embellishment of Steph's faults by a disgruntled husband; she imagined the woman to be evil incarnate.

They gutted the upstairs bathroom, allowing her a share in the demolition, an unexpectedly satisfying act. There's a pleasure about destruction that runs deep in the human core. Then they furred-out the exterior wall from a four inch stud-wall to a six inch stud-wall, to add insulation.

This was all new to Phia, and she liked that it distracted her from her rough past and her non-existent future. Although she had not put carpentry on her secret bucket list, it found a place there by default.

She was applying mud to the bathroom wall seams and screws with the last dabs of joint compound in the bucket. Aaron was out buying more.

She heard street noise swell through the opening front door and diminish with the closing. "Good timing," she called. "I'm just about out."

The light sound of footsteps stopped at the bathroom door and a woman's voice said, "Out where?"

Phia turned to see a slim, blond woman, six inches taller and five years older than herself. "Who are you?" Phia asked.

"I own this house. Who are *you*?"

"Really? I haven't seen you around here driving nails."

Steph gave Phia the once over, down and up. The old, baggy overalls, handed down from Aaron, did not enhance Phia's figure, but the gaping suspenders allowed a good view of her tight tank-top. "Now I see," Steph said, "why the Giffin boys spend so much time at this crappy place. I'd say they're nailing more than just boards."

Steph had made a bad start with Phia. Though it was true that Phia had suggested a fair-trade arrangement with Aaron, he had declined, and they were being unjustly accused. Her back stiffened, her eyes became slits, then she relaxed slowly and smiled up at Steph. "You must be Stephanie. I heard about you and your so, *so* sweet personality."

Angered by the mere presence of Phia in this house, and the idea of Aaron revealing god-knows-what marital secrets to the little viper, Steph spat, "Bitch."

Phia said, "Woof woof."

"Whore!"

Phia did her best to emulate a curtsy, like in the movies. When she straightened she said, still smiling, "You know me pretty good. Now you'll call me 'cunt' and be at the end of your list of insults. Since you're done, get the hell out. The mud's gettin' dry."

Steph sputtered, "You don't know who you're dealing with! I get a big chunk of this place when the divorce goes through!"

Phia cocked her head at Steph. Her face went blank. She looked down as she raised the sharp corner of the mudding trowel to the flesh of her forearm, stabbed through the skin and drew it up, leaving a trail of running blood. Phia raised her dull eyes to the horrified Steph and said quietly, "You don't know who *you're* dealing with." Then she lifted the bloody, muddy trowel in Steph's direction.

The front door slammed open, but didn't close. Phia walked out to shut it, listening to the racing engine fading down the block. She slowly returned from the flattened world of her safe place, and chuckled as she went looking for the first-aid kit. This was the best she had felt in years.

When Aaron asked her about the bandage, she told him that she had dropped the trowel and tried to catch it, but missed.

Daniel Peterson

8. Phia and Aaron

The room was barely big enough for both to apply paint, but they avoided collision. And when it came down to a one person job, Phia stepped outside to watch Aaron finish.

"See any misses?" Aaron asked, craning around to get advantageous light on the ceiling and walls. One of the fiscal corners they decided to cut was in paint. They selected one, general purpose, light color and used it everywhere. This saved time and labor. It also made a good base for the future owners to re-paint in colors suiting their tastes.

"No. Looks good. Here, give me that." She took his paint roller and hers, and the touch-up brushes, down to the utility sink in the laundry. Aaron poured the paint remnant from the roller pan into the paint can and sealed the can. Then he took the pan down to join Phia.

With the tools cleaned and set aside to dry, Aaron said, "Want to give me a hand buying insulation and sheet rock for the bedroom?"

"Sure."

The bedroom that had served as the kitchen was next on the list. The last occupants of the house must have led a tumultuous home life; there were large cracks in the walls and the hollow-core door with shoe prints centered in them. Splits radiated from the doorknob, and the doorjamb was splintered were the striker plate had torn out.

On the quiet drive across town in Aaron's truck, Phia admitted, "I wasn't honest the other day. I should have told you your wife came by."

"I heard. You made a real impression."

Phia frowned, "I almost impressed her face with my fist."

After a long pause Aaron said, "You know, I might have exaggerated Steph's faults. She used to be different. Just the last year or so she got pretty tense. I think she expected more from our marriage."

"More than what? More than a good man? She doesn't know how good she had it."

"Good man, *Rhea*?"

"Yes, *Adam*."

They shared smiles at the newly-minted, private joke.

Back at the house, they packed the insulation rolls into the living room, stacking them in a corner, then they carried in the gypsum board, each taking an end of the paired sheets, and leaned them against a wall. They brought in armloads of the boards for furring strips.

The next step was continuing the demolition begun in anger by the previous owners.

Phia, at the breaker box in the basement, turned off and, after a pause, back on, one unlabeled switch at a time until the lamp in the bedroom went out. Aaron shouted, "That's it," and Phia stopped flipping switches.

Phia joined Aaron upstairs and they took off all of the outlet covers and retaining screws, pulling each fixture out to stand on straightened wires.

They pried at the trim around the windows. The wood wasn't salvageable so they did not handle it gently.

As Phia snapped one long piece loose, a big spider scurried out of the exposed gap between window frame and wall, skittering across the wall toward her in its confusion. She backed away shrieking, "Spider! Kill it!"

Aaron reached over, brushed it off the wall, said, "Sorry, Bud," and stepped on it.

She looked at him oddly. "Why did you do that?"

"You wanted me to."

"No. Why did you apologize?"

"Did I?"

"Yeah. You said, 'Sorry, Bud' before you squashed it."

He thought back. "Well, it was alive, just like us. If it hadn't been in the wrong place at the wrong time, I would still *be* alive."

"You would?"

"What?"

"You said, '*I* would still be alive'."

"*It* would. *It*."

She studied him. "You," she said, "are really a funny guy."

He turned back to his work.

They started removing drywall at opposite ends of the exterior walls. They smashed through the sheet rock with hammers, gripped the rough edge and yanked so the nails either pulled out with the wallboard or tore through. Whatever ragged pieces broke loose they tossed behind them into the center of the room.

They built a good sweat.

Through the dust in the close room, Phia could smell Aaron. She took a whiff of herself and realized he could probably sense her.

He noticed. He ignored. Compared to the travel effluvium she sported that first night when he undressed her, this was perfume. Aaron was glad his armpit smell had not reached the level which it sometimes did, of aged tomcat piss.

They pulled the old nails, tossing the bent remains into empty joint compound buckets at their feet. Phia thought they got an amazing lot of good use from old joint compound buckets. After a careful check for missed nails, they hauled all of the scrap trim and broken sheet rock out to Aaron's truck, swept the floor and drove the waste to the local transfer station.

When they returned, Nick was there, arrived from his day job, now in overalls and dust mask, carefully pulling staples, removing strips of fiberglass insulation and stacking it on the floor in the closet. They all took a short supper break.

Setting aside the dirty dinnerware, they returned to the bedroom. Aaron told Phia, "Go put on a long-sleeved shirt."

"Too warm."

"Better warm than itchy. Voice of experience."

She cocked her head dubiously but nodded and retreated to her bedroom to find a shirt. When she came back, he handed her a dust mask, gloves, and one of his ball caps tightened to fit her head. With all three working, it only took a few minutes to remove the rest of the insulation and set it aside for later re-installation.

Nick set the table saw to rip furring strips. Aaron helped Nick rip the first five boards, then Aaron and Phia returned to the bedroom where Aaron measured the length for the first furring strip and called the number out to Nick, who repeated it, measured along the freshly ripped board and cut it to length. Aaron called out the next length. Phia fetched the newly cut strip and helped hold it in position while Aaron placed the first nail with the stud nailer. Nick cut the next strip, Phia fetched it while Aaron completed the nailing—bang, bang, bang—and the cycle continued.

Phia and Aaron worked in an intricate dance where the rule seemed to be one of near misses, the dancers required to come as close as possible to each other in awkward poses while never actually contacting, then withdrawing to a discrete distance and pretending that they had not nearly touched. Occasionally they did touch. At these, Aaron would twitch away. Phia noticed this and ignored it at first. Then it amused her when it kept happening. Then she arranged to touch him more frequently, and would lean closer as he twitched away, regaining contact. He pulled away further, sometimes precariously balanced. Finally Phia smiled and pushed him so that he stumbled away trying to keep his feet.

"What are you doing?" he asked.

"What are *you* doing? You afraid of me? You've already undressed me once. And I don't have lice."

"Just trying to give you space."

"When I need more space I'll take it. Relax."

He studied her mocking smile, shrugged and said, "Grab the next strip."

As they resumed in close proximity, Phia breathed Aaron's musky scent, mingled now with the tang of fresh sawdust. It was a strangely comforting combination, engendering a sense of home and place, and raising a longing for a past which could have included such a place.

But she had never lived in a real home, or known her father, and doubted he ever smelled of sawdust—booze, yes, but not sawdust. The boys and men she had clung to out of necessity smelled sour, casually unclean, never of fresh work sweat, and certainly never sawdust.

She peeked at Aaron—generous, calm, confident and capable. All of those past males were losers, low-lifes, or just broken inside. Even the few nice guys that she knew were damaged beyond repair. Aaron was a rock, and he smelled good.

It was late enough when they finished that they did not start moving the electrical boxes. Nick went home, leaving the other two cleaning the mess in the living room. After cleanup they each showered, then sat with a couple of beers to watch a streaming video on Aaron's laptop computer.

Phia stood and stretched as the closing credits played.

"Oh!" she said. "I got stiff today."

"I thought you'd be beyond that by now."

"This stuff is hard work."

"You'll get used to it. Take an aspirin. Get some rest."

"You too. G'night." She walked down the basement steps, used the toilet, washed, brushed her teeth, scanned her cot for spiders and climbed in. She heard Aaron descend the steps, use the bathroom and return upstairs. She lay for a while before sleep, thinking about him lying up there alone, and recalled his musk-and-sawdust smell. Unsuspected by Phia, Aaron mused similarly about her, recalling her playful mockery of their incidental touching. They both pushed this foolishness out of mind, he by thinking about the work scheduled for tomorrow and she by wondering if she would wake up tomorrow.

Aaron removed the old outlets and boxes. Phia watched, learning what she could, but was dubious about ever performing electrical work herself; electricity scared her. The quiet lesson was enough effort for her; the previous evening's stiffness had become this morning's aches. Another aspirin and light work limbered her up.

The day became unusually warm for late September, and the low sun through the bedroom windows pumped in even more heat.

After a lunch of ham-and-cheese sandwiches, they put on dust masks and, despite the heat, long sleeved shirts. They opened a bundle of insulation. Aaron measured the height of the first stud bay and Phia cut the insulation with rusty, antique sheep shears which Aaron had sharpened with a few strokes of a file.

They stapled the last insulation by three o'clock and, after a short break, measured for the first piece of sheet rock. They cut, placed and screwed rock to studs, one, two, more. Their sweat the previous day paled by comparison with the swampy flow they produced now, rolling off them in a tepid slick. On the sixth drywall sheet, a flimsy piece between the corner and a window, Aaron held the part in position with a level along the edge while Phia prepared to start the first screw.

He reached over her head to adjust the sheet. Her nose hovered near his armpit. His odor had crossed that line to tomcat piss.

"Whoa!" she said.

"Sorry. I did shower this morning."

"You worked it off. Wow."

"It happens. You want to set that screw?"

"Okay."

Phia ran in the low screws while Aaron set the high ones. When the sheet was secured, he said, "I think I'll go down and get another shower."

"Don't stop work on my account. It's not going to kill me. I been around worse. Hell, I've *been* worse. You know that."

"Thing is, I'd like to shed the fiberglass prickles around my neck anyway. I'll be back."

"What you want me to do?"

"Take a break."

He picked clean clothes from his bedroom and went downstairs. He undressed, adjusted the shower, stepped in, closed the stall door and got wet. The bathroom door opened, then the stall door, and a small, naked woman joined him in the confined space.

"I'm feeling prickly, too," Phia said.

Aaron hesitated, then slipped around the stall to let her into the shower stream. They soaped each other, rubbed at the smelly bits and rinsed off. Aaron shut off the water and they continued rubbing at some of the formerly smelly bits. They felt cramped in the stall so they stepped out and Phia grabbed a condom packet from the sink rim where she had left it.

"Glad you brought that," Aaron said as she applied it. "I don't have any."

"Had to learn young."

They resumed where they had left off, getting their stride back and finishing with vigor.

"I need a shower," Aaron said, breathing heavily.

"Me too."

They stepped back in for a quick rinse.

Out of the stall again they were drying each other when Phia faced his front, jumped up and clamped her legs around his hips, clinging to his neck with her arms, tucking her head beside his jaw. He supported her damp rump with one hand and cradled her head with the other, waiting to see what came next.

Muffled against his neck, Phia said, "I never thanked you for taking me in, so thanks. You been great."

"Is that what the shower was about? I told you before..."

"No! The shower was to finish our silly touch and go game."

And it was a means of laying claim to him and coercing his loyalty as female primates have done for a million years, though she didn't know it's what she did. She had survived that way for so long, it was reflex.

Aaron said, "Okay, it was fun. But I'm not ready to jump into a new relationship. Just letting you know. Don't want you hurt."

She leaned back to look in his face. "You didn't hear me say 'ouch'."

"You know what I mean."

"Yeah. I know the score. What about you? You gonna get hurt?"

"Not likely. You scare me."

She dropped off his hips and stood smiling up at him with her hands on his chest. "You like it."

"But it'll make me paranoid."

"I won't be here long enough for that."

"Why not? You're good help."

She saddened. "Sure," she said and left the bathroom to dress.

9. Phia, Aaron and Nick

"Hey, Giffin boys," Phia said two evenings later. "Could you front me some cash? My phone bill is due."

Aaron and Nick looked at each other. "Sure," Aaron said. "You and I can run by the bank tomorrow and I'll transfer some to your account."

"And I'll take time out tomorrow to look for work, if you can spare me."

"No problem. You know we'd like to pay you, but it isn't in the budget."

"No. I'm eating free and learning a lot. That's enough. I'll get work."

"Up to you."

"By the way," Phia said. "How did you guys learn all this?"

Nick said, "Dad. He's a general contractor. We helped build our parents' house when we were teenagers."

That evening the men worked on the bathroom. Nick set tile above the tub in the surround, while Aaron measured and started cutting parts for the new cabinet. They had decided that the old tub was still good enough, and it would save money to re-use it. Phia applied the first layer of joint compound in the bedroom.

The next morning, Aaron and Phia went to the bank, Phia following Aaron's truck in her car, now cleaned out, vacuumed, wiped down, and boasting a retro, tree-shaped air freshener dangling from the mirror. She was still running on the tank of fuel bought in Lewiston weeks ago. They settled on two hundred dollars as a reasonable sum and a clerk made the transfer to Phia's account in Des Moines. During the process, Aaron finally learned Phia's last name: Marshall.

The transfer would have been a telltale to anyone trying to locate Phia, but nobody went to the police with a missing person report when she disappeared. Some of her acquaintances were concerned; occasional texts, diminished in frequency, still popped up from one of them, but none of them had much desire to approach the police about anything. Many were engaged in minor illegalities and some already boasted criminal records. Nobody saw her leave, and there were rumors of blood all over the kitchen floor at Junior's house, and Junior dropped from view around the same time. Knowing Junior's volatility, some assumed he killed her, got rid of the body and ran. But that was just rumor. And if it was true, there would be no point in getting the police looking for a missing person who was already dead.

After the bank, Phia made the rounds of the bars, looking for work. It's what she knew.

As he left the bank, Aaron received a text message that his lawyer wanted to see him, so he went to the law office. The lawyer told him that Stephanie was now including mental and emotional abuse and mental cruelty to her accusations, and starting a civil suit above and beyond any settlement which might be reached in the divorce. This could give her all of Aaron's share in the house, the lion's share of money in their savings, and long term payments. He wondered what happened to Steph over the last year to make her so grasping and vindictive. His lawyer thought Stephanie would have difficulty proving her allegations. Aaron was not reassured.

He went home, considering how to go on from there. He wondered if there was any point in continuing the remodel knowing that it was possible he would never get a return. He lacked the grit at the moment to work on the bathroom cabinet, so he tossed chicken and vegetables in the crock-pot for supper. Then he went for a long walk.

"That bitch!" Phia exclaimed at supper when Aaron told her and Nick what his lawyer had revealed.

"Damn," Nick said. "I used to like Steph. What got into her?"

"No idea. Early onset Alzheimer's?"

"At twenty eight?"

"Maybe her lawyer, trying to pad his fee."

They ate for a while. "By the way," Nick said. "Good stew."

Aaron smiled sarcastically. "Thanks. Slaved all day over a hot slow-cooker."

They put in a short, lackluster evening's work and Nick went home. He was not looking forward to telling Patty about the latest development in Aaron's troubles; she was not keen on the house project and remained sympathetic to Stephanie.

That night, after Aaron and Phia retired to their beds, Phia rose again, climbed the stairs and slipped into Aaron's room. She joined him in bed and cuddled tight. Aaron closed an accepting arm across her.

"It'll be okay," she said. "There's no way she can win the suit."

"That's what the lawyer said. But how did Steph turn so

mean? Until she walked out, I thought things were going to be fine, that she'd calm down when we sold this place. Now, if she wins the case, Nick and I won't have the money to start the next house unless I hit the fire lines again. Puts us years behind."

"Forget it. Let me give you something else to think about."

And she did.

Thereafter, Phia slept in Aaron's bed, abandoning her downstairs room and the spiders.

Phia found a job working evening shift at a sports bar called Huevos, so she began replenishing her account. Her days were still free to help Aaron, who decided there was no point in just sitting around waiting for the ax to fall. They might as well do something constructive, even if it eventually went for nothing. They resumed the remodel, though with less joy.

Thoughts came to Phia over the next week. She liked these Giffin boys. They treated her well, and they were the first men in her life to do so reliably. She had now met two men at the same time who completely revised her idea of what all men are. So she liked them. And she owed them a lot, not just for the new perspective, but also for taking her into their lives without prejudice, and for teaching her useful new skills that only required lying on her back while addressing a non-biological variety of plumbing. Now she knew how to replace a sink.

They did not demand, nor value, sex as payment, which presented a dilemma. In what way could she repay them if her usual trade goods had lost cachet?

Two days later, sorting laundry, she picked up a piece of paper from the bedroom floor and read it. It was a communication forwarded through Aaron's lawyer concerning the lawsuit, which included the name of Stephanie's lawyer, and the present home address of Stephanie Giffin.

Stephanie. What about Stephanie? The greatest encumbrance on Aaron's life and happiness was Stephanie. If Phia could solve that problem, it would be a good deed for a good man. But what could Phia do? She couldn't sit the woman down for a heart-to-heart talk and persuade her to drop the civil suit; Steph despised Phia. And probably feared Phia. Hmm, maybe intimidation was the key. A realistic threat of bodily harm might straighten Stephanie out. Phia had led a rough life, so she was not above extortion. She could corner Steph somewhere with a baseball bat and have a chat. If the chat alone didn't work, she could catch her again and apply a few bruises, maybe a broken arm, for reinforcement. No, if Steph went to the police or, worse, Aaron, Phia's effort would be foiled and she would be thrown out of her comfortable situation without any gain for Aaron. Steph would have to be effectively and permanently warned off without knowing who did it, but how could that be done?

The Giffins and Phia kept at the work in the bath and bedroom.

Tuesday, mid-afternoon, Aaron unbuckled his tool belt and said. "Let's get cleaned up."

"Why?"

"We've been at this long enough. Time for a break. We're going out for a nice meal and the latest 3-D blockbuster."

"Like a date?"

Aaron blushed. "No, like time off."

"Just curious. Kind of late to start dating. Considering the regular sex and all."

"You going to make a big deal out of this?"

She smiled. "Come on—toughen up. A movie is great. Not *Rocky 15*, I hope."

He smiled back. "No, *Star Wars 16.*"

"Ooo, *The Empire Strikes Out*."

Aaron laughed. "Yeah, they trade light sabers for bats."

"Cool. Let's shower."

At work the next day, refreshed and encouraged by the evening out, Phia began to fantasize about ways to permanently dispose of Steph. And who better to perpetrate the perfect murder than Phia, a person destined to die in less time than a sickly dog? Phia feared nothing from police, criminal courts, prisons, nor even the death penalty. The perfection lay in not even needing to get away with it; she would die before the courts ground through to dealing with her.

The process would be simple. She could just walk up to the bitch and beat her to death with a club, or cut her throat, or, to make the job more certain and easier for Phia, find a gun to shoot Stephanie from a discrete distance, say, three feet given her lack of experience with guns. When the authorities came to arrest her, she could either surrender calmly and wait for the aneurysm to take her away or shoot herself in the head.

For three days, Phia searched for an alternative but could think of nothing better, so she went shopping. Aaron didn't ask for details. A woman's shopping is an activity for which no experienced male will seek reason.

After visiting gun outlets and pawn shops she chose a little Kel-Tec P-32 semi-automatic. Even for this used pistol at the pawn shop, the cost nearly erased her bank account. Despite her association with known felons in Des Moines, she was never convicted or even arrested for a felony. A week later she returned to pick up her new pistol and then stopped at a sporting goods store for a box of ammunition. She could drop the gun in a pocket if she chose and carry it legally almost anywhere in Idaho.

Even at this juncture, Phia searched for options besides murder. But she did not consider what her plans said about her own mental and emotional state, or how her broken past made murder appear a reasonable act.

Aaron noticed her distraction.

"You okay?" he asked

"Sorry, just daydreaming. I'll concentrate."

But three days along she still could think of no more effective solution than a couple of bullets to the brain. She could at least make a dry run to test the possibility.

That evening, Phia finished her work shift, started home, but stopped at an all-night place called Burger Excess, at one-thirty-eight in the morning. She was hungry. She pulled up to the drive-through intercom. Nothing on the menu looked like it could satisfy her hunger. Then she realized that it was a different hunger, a hunger to get on with her plan to help the Giffins. She drove on through the drive-through, and turned right.

The town was still unfamiliar, so it took time to locate Stephanie's neighborhood. She slowly drove through a green traffic light, trying to read the darkened street signs, when a Ford Mustang, ignoring its red light, raced through the intersection, narrowly missed Phia's Metro, swiped the curb and roared away up the street.

"Damned drunks!" Phia yelled, flipping off the receding car.

She pulled over to let her adrenaline burn out, and to stop shaking. But the jolt also gave her an angry edginess, a spur to get on with the job.

She found Steph's house, parked outside the cul-de-sac, pulled her pistol out of the glove box, and walked to the door.

Stephanie obviously wouldn't answer the doorbell at this time of night, would she? And if she did, a gunshot at the front door might rouse the neighbors. Phia walked around the side of the house. The back door into the kitchen was unlocked. She eased it open. It didn't creak. The house smelled of well used cat litter, which hopefully meant no dog. Distant streetlamps dimly illuminated the kitchen and the arched passage out to the dining nook on the far side. She turned left there, noting the living room at her left and a hallway to the right. Carpeting muffled her light steps, and a mild creak of floor boards, as she approached the hall and looked into it. There was a closet with sliding doors and three other doorways—two bedrooms and a bath. She paused. Until now she hadn't thought of the possibility that Steph would have a housemate, but wouldn't that be likely since her abrupt departure from Aaron would require dunning a charitable friend or relative? Even if she initially stayed at a motel, she would have found cheaper, shared, housing. Phia couldn't hear any sounds of sleeping people.

She crept along the hall, noting that the first door was the bath, then looked around the next doorjamb on her left. An unoccupied bed, but a bed which had been used if the rumpled covers meant anything. There did not seem to be an attached bathroom, so the occupant must be out of the house. At two in the morning?

She proceeded to the next door. Gentle exhalations sighed from the room, where she discerned the long mound of a person in the bed.

This was not good. If this was Steph, Phia could just walk up, put the gun to her head and be done. But if this was the innocent roommate, Phia was stymied. She had worked herself up to commit murder for Aaron, but not randomly kill everybody in her way. Leaving a spare corpse around the house for Steph to find would not make it easier to reach her. Nor could Phia wake this person up for identification. That would be fine if it was Stephanie, but, if not, the person would be terrorized to no purpose, and perhaps recognize Phia later, which would interfere with her plan for Stephanie.

A large cat lying on the foot of the bed, visible only as a lighter lump, growled at Phia. She backed down the hall. A siren wailed in the distance. She wondered if there was a silent intrusion alarm here, and if the police would be hauling her away with her mission unfinished. She couldn't risk arrest; the delay might allow her aneurysm to fail, leaving her dead and Aaron no better off.

Phia turned and hurried out. As she drove down the street, an ambulance shrieked by in the opposite direction. Oh, well, she thought. Maybe next time.

Aaron muttered as she crawled in beside him. "It's late. You okay?"

"Fine. Go back to sleep." She absorbed what he had said. Aaron was worried about her. There was a little ruffle of new feeling high in her chest, tightening her throat. He was worried about her. Very few people ever worried about her, and none whom she considered worth a shit. But he was worried. She fell asleep relishing that warm ruffle.

Near noon the following morning Aaron's phone rang. Phia watched him listen as his face changed from annoyance to alarm.

"What? You're kidding. What happened?" he asked. He listened.

"Oh god. She must be crazier than I thought. Will she be okay?" He shook his head at what he heard.

"Okay. What room is she in?"

Pause.

"Thanks. I'll run over." He pressed "end" and looked up at Phia.

She raised her brows.

"That was about Steph. She went out last night, got drunk, drove home, missed a corner and wrecked her Mustang. She's in the hospital. I gotta go see her."

"Mustang?" Phia asked. Apparently both she and her nemesis experienced close calls at the hands of the other without knowing.

Aaron nodded, unbuckled his tool belt and hung it on the end of a sawhorse.

"Want me to come?" Phia asked.

Aaron looked thoughtful, but shook his head. "I doubt that would cheer her up." He smiled. "No offense."

She shrugged. "I can use the time to clean up around here and start supper. Good luck."

Aaron left. Phia began picking up wood scraps, tossing them into the big box labeled "Wood Scraps Only".

The situation with Steph gave her food for thought. First, she was glad that she didn't shoot the person she found where Steph lived. Then, how would this affect Phia's plan to help the Giffins? If Steph died, that would take care of the problem. If not, Phia would have to think about how to reach her. Actually, with Steph in the hospital, the uncertainty Phia encountered at the house would be gone. All she would have to do is walk through the hospital to her room in full daylight, go up to her bed, pull the pistol and shoot her in the face. But she didn't have to make specific plans until after Aaron came home and apprised her of the situation.

Before Aaron came back, Phia left for work. And she put the pistol in her car's glove box.

Aaron was already gone the next morning when Phia rolled out of bed. A note lay on the kitchen counter beside the coffee pot which explained that Steph would recover from her injuries, but that she would need help for a week or two.

Phia drank her coffee, re-reading the note and considering its implications. She took a shower, made herself breakfast, and got on her phone.

"Hey," Aaron answered.

"Hey. Where you at?"

"Helping Steph get out of the hospital."

"Glad to hear she's okay. What's the plan?"

"I'll get her back to Becky's place. Then..." he hesitated.

"Then?"

"I'll take the basement cot. You're not using it anymore. I'll set it up in Becky's living room so I can take care of Steph."

"Okay," Phia said neutrally.

"She's still my wife."

Phia frowned, but said, "True. I didn't expect you to do any different." But to herself she thought, this puts a twist in my plan for Steph.

"You sound weird."

"Bad link. You'll be by later?"

"Yeah. See you then."

"Before I leave for work?"

"Yup. Hour from now. Two at most."

Phia went into the bedroom. She threw herself onto their bed with her face sunk in Aaron's pillow and breathed his smell.

After a few minutes, she mentally kicked herself. "Better lend a hand," she said out loud, rolling off the bed and walking down to the basement bedroom. She stripped the sheets from the cot. They and other random dirty laundry went into the washer, with the pillowcase from her pillow. She stripped the case off of Aaron's pillow and slipped it onto hers without washing. She also dug one of his soiled tee-shirts out of the laundry and hid it under her pillow. It would comfort her to have his scent while he was gone.

She rolled the camping pad. Folding the clumsy cot was a struggle, but she succeeded and carried it up to the living room with the pad. It seemed best to leave packing Aaron's clothes to him. To pack for him was not only prone to error, but an intrusion to his personal space which he might not feel she could take.

The sheets, lying folded on the compacted cot by the door, were warm from the dryer when Aaron came in. He saw them and looked around for Phia. Her car was still outside, so she was here somewhere. He walked into the bedroom where she lay curled on the bed.

"You awake?" he whispered.

"Of course," she said, opening her eyes.

"Thanks for getting the gear ready."

"Just trying to help." She sat up on the edge of the bed. "I left the clothes packing to you."

"That's fine." He pulled his duffle out of the closet, lay it on the bed and started stuffing it with clothes. He looked at Phia in passing. "Still have a bad link? You sound a little strange."

"I'm just sad your going."

"I'll be back in two weeks."

"Will you? Stephanie might wise up after you get her through this, and take you back."

"But it takes two. Even if she changed her mind, why would I risk it?"

Phia shrugged.

Aaron sat beside her, put his arm around her and said, "Don't look so lost. Everything will turn out."

"Things always do, always bad."

Aaron considered that. "Did you figure the situation here, you and me, was going somewhere?"

"No. But I hoped it would last a while."

"Its been good, hasn't it?"

"Better than I deserve. I don't even know how I got here. Feel like a weed in the Garden of Eden."

"There are no weeds in Eden. You're a wild rose. You have some thorns, but you're not a weed."

She made a small smile. "It'll be a dull garden without you."

"I'll be back in two weeks. Bet on it. Maybe Steph will even come to her senses and drop the civil suit."

Phia looked up at him with a peculiar expression, like she still had trouble with that link. She said, "That would be real good."

10. Aaron and Steph

Aaron received a spare key from Becky when he arrived at her place earlier that day delivering the patched-up Stephanie. He rented a wheel chair from a small medical device store in the annex beside the hospital. Even if Stephanie was not too battered to walk, she was too highly dosed with pain medication to manage it. Wheeling his wife into the house was not a simple feat, either. There was no ramp, and it was surprisingly difficult even with big wheels to hoist a one-hundred-twenty pound woman up a step at a time for three steps. He rolled Steph to her bedroom and helped her carefully transfer to the newly cleaned and made bed. After making sure that her immediate needs were supplied—her phone and charger, the video remotes, a water glass with a straw—Aaron assured her that he would return soon.

Steph had been barely responsive to Aaron since he arrived at the hospital. He was not sure whether it was the drugs or the ill-will she still felt toward him.

When he returned with the cot, he checked on Stephanie, who seemed comfortable but ignored him, then he set up the cot in the living room.

Aaron went back into Steph's room. "Can I get you anything? Soup? More pain pills?"

She shook her head without looking at him. The television was on, tuned to a wildlife show.

Aaron asked, "Would you like me to read to you?" He was a good reader. This was an activity they used to enjoy together, and a task she couldn't do for herself now because the cast on her broken hand and arm did not allow manipulation of a book, which she preferred over an e-reader.

She shook her head again.

"Okay, I'll leave you alone. But I'll be in the living room. Call me if you need something."

Two hours later Steph called Aaron's name. He set aside the book he was reading and went to help her sit up, swing off the bed and transfer to the wheel chair. The hall was barely wide enough to maneuver down to the bathroom and in. The chair would go through the doorway but could not be taken further because it would block the toilet. This meant that Aaron must go in backward first, pulling the chair and Steph through the door, and then assist Steph out of the chair and onto the toilet, pausing in mid-transfer to pull down her pajama bottoms. For the last actions, he stood with one foot in the bathtub.

Stephanie was never shy about bodily functions while they lived together, but now she gestured him out toward the hall. He pushed the chair through, closing the door behind him.

Later, returned to the bed and covered, she said, "I'm getting hungry."

"I'm on it."

In ten minutes he returned and presented her a deep mug of tomato soup with a straw, which she took in her good hand.

She thanked him. He sat on the edge of the bed.

"I can handle it," she said.

Aaron stood back up and left her to her meal.

On the third day, after she received her supper of chicken broth and apple juice, as Aaron turned to go, Steph said,

"You can stay if you want." There was not a string of concerned friends parading through, and she was lonely.

"Sure." He sat on the bed. "You feeling better?"

"Some. How do I look?"

Aaron smiled mildly. "Don't look in the mirror yet."

"That's what I was afraid of."

He watched her eat awhile, then asked, "Steph, what made you want to get that drunk?"

"I don't want to talk about it."

"But..."

"No!"

"Okay."

She sipped her broth. "How's my car?"

"Totaled. And there are traffic citations you'll have to deal with when you're back up and around."

"My car," she said sadly. "I loved that car."

Daniel Peterson

11. Phia and Nick

Progress crawled at the house. Phia's days off were Monday and Tuesday. Nick's days off were Thursday and Friday. Phia left for work in late afternoon. Nick either arrived shortly after, and sat down for a moment to eat, or stopped by his apartment to eat with Patty, then showed at the house later. He put in four or five hours on the remodel, and went home. Phia came back around one-thirty in the morning, took a glimpse at Nick's progress for the day and went to bed.

In the mornings Phia found a note by the coffeepot listing jobs she could tackle, though usually this only amounted to cleanup. She ate breakfast, took a closer look at what Nick had accomplished, and worked at her appointed tasks. She always finished well ahead of her time to leave for work, so she became more bored each day, spending much of her time watching streaming video on Aaron's laptop computer. She called Aaron frequently, but there was little to discuss beyond the daily progress of Steph, which annoyed Phia, and daily progress at the house, which frustrated Aaron. Then she showered, dressed and went to work, completing the cycle.

Phia thought about going over to see Aaron, maybe make his cot squawk if he was willing, but when she spoke of it, he discouraged the plan. He didn't think Phia's presence in the house would enhance Stephanie's peace-of-mind. And making the cot squawk would drive her crazy even if it did not collapse under the strain.

On Nick's days off, he accomplished marvels. He put in fifteen hour days, and Aaron broke away from Steph for short

85

periods to look at the progress and to hobnob with his brother. Aaron was careful not to overstay, because if Steph needed something while he was gone it rankled her to be ignored in favor of the hated house.

On Phia's days off, she helped Nick, but she hardly boosted progress.

Phia felt she was living in a haunted house. The signs of Nick's activities were everywhere, while she rarely caught a glimpse of the man. She wondered if he might also think of her as a ghostly figure dabbling around the house while he was gone, especially since her impact was less substantial than his.

12. Aaron and Steph

Steph's aching face healed enough to eat with a spoon. Aaron brought her a bowl of oatmeal.

"I can't wait to bite into steak," Steph said.

"Won't be long now. You're doin' great."

Steph looked at him in a way that she hadn't for nearly a year. "Aaron, I appreciate you being here, doing this."

He shrugged. "You're my wife. I can't shuck off six years like they didn't mean anything."

She spooned oatmeal while he watched. She swallowed, breathed and said, "I was losing control."

"What?"

"Actually, I lost control. You asked about getting drunk and wrecking my poor Mustang. It was frustration and fear."

"What do you have to be afraid of?"

"A future I couldn't make. That's what drove me over the brink with you and that house. Before the house, we had regular income, we were saving money. We could have built our own house some day. Have the kids we talked about. But you threw all that away and there was nothing I could do about it. I had no say in my own life. So I did the only thing I could."

"I showed you the numbers. It will work."

"Those numbers don't mean anything. You can't predict the market next spring. Housing could take another dive and you'll be bankrupt."

"The limited partnership protects us. We could get through that. Besides, the market's as likely to boom as bust."

Steph shook her head. "It's too big a risk. And I couldn't make you see. You couldn't hear me. I had no say in my own life."

"Everything is a risk. You lost your job, and what could you do about that? Worry more? Life is a risk."

"I need stability. Drinking didn't help that, I know. But there's one thing alcohol can do. It can give me a say."

"How? In what?"

"Alcohol kills ambition. When I drink, all the dreams, goals and ambitions, they're gone. But at least I'm *choosing* to destroy my *own* ambitions instead of somebody else killing them. Like you did!"

He looked at her as if she was a stranger. Was he like that? Did he really do that to her? "I...I'm sorry. I didn't... It just seemed like... I don't know. I had no idea you felt like that. Maybe I could have explained better."

"No. I'm just not built for it. I'm sorry I dropped it on you like a bomb, but I hit my limit. I panicked."

He digested this for a long while. Then, sighing and shaking his head, he said, "Steph, you can only be you, like, I guess, I can only be me. Are you still going ahead with the divorce? Not going to move into the house with the sawdust, noise and paint fumes?" He chuckled to indicate levity.

She smiled darkly. "That house can burn to the ground for all I care. The divorce stands. Besides, I see how you look at me. The spark is gone. I guess that's my fault. You wouldn't take me back now if I begged. And you have your little girlfriend." He opened his mouth to respond, and she raised a deflecting hand. "But I'm dropping the civil suit. That was beyond my control, too, with the lawyer hounding me. A good lawyer, but a mean man."

Aaron looked down at his hands, thought about clarifying Phia's status, and found he couldn't. He wasn't sure he understood it himself. He looked back at Steph. "What'll you do now?"

"I guess I have to pull myself together and start over. Get a job, stability. My panic only made things worse." Then she closed her eyes, pinched the bridge of her nose with her good hand and moaned, "I don't even have a car anymore."

"I'll help."

She dropped her hand from her face, balled up a fistful of bed covers, and looked up. "I know," she said wryly. "That's how you're made."

Daniel Peterson

13. Phia, Aaron and Nick

It was early November when Nick and Phia finished the bathroom. This was an accomplishment because the kitchen and bathroom are the two most demanding rooms to remodel, but it fell far short of their intended time-line. While waiting for Aaron's return, they began demolishing the dining room.

Aaron, good to his word, returned "home" to Phia after two weeks. They felt subtle tensions in the house through the following week; Aaron only now felt the finality and reality of his impending divorce because of the constant, intimate, and emotionally distant time with his wife, but he was also uneasy with Phia, feeling a vague disloyalty to Steph at leaping back into bed with Phia. Phia allowed him his peace through the week, not pushing for intimacy.

She was relieved at the news that Steph was withdrawing the civil suit. She was glad she didn't have to murder the woman, but it left her searching again for a means to repay the Giffins. So perhaps it was too early to entirely discard the option of killing Steph; the divorce could potentially ruin the boys. While awaiting developments in that arena, she started paying them a token monthly rent of one hundred fifty dollars.

At the beginning of the second week after Aaron's return home, Phia, the Giffins and Patty, who had felt neglected since the remodel began, went out to the Fleidermaus to celebrate the bathroom with pizza and beer.

Aaron said to Phia, "You're not going to repeat your last

performance here, right?"

"No. Life was crappy then. Can I have a Black Butte Porter, boss?"

"You earned it."

Aaron ordered a pitcher of lager for Nick, Patty and himself. They drank slowly, awaiting the pizza and making small talk.

While pouring the second beer, Nick said, "Phia, you never told us about you. All we know is you're from Des Moines. You always live there?"

Phia was not proud of her past, even the bits over which she had no control. She did not want to distress Aaron with knowing she could drop dead on him at any moment. But maybe they deserved to know a little about her, at least in return for the openness they'd shown her. She was beginning to trust the boys. They were good people. If they didn't want her around because of a sketchy past, so-be-it; she'd get in her car and continue west.

"Yeah, born and raised there, if 'raised' covers all that crap. Not sure how much you want to hear, or I want to tell."

"Up to you," Aaron said.

"Okay. I'll keep it short.

"Mom never wanted me. She didn't care which of the men she screwed was my father. Usual shit while I was still with her. Abused by two assholes that 'dated' her. Dirty all the time, short on sleep, hungry, living on their cigarette smoke and pizza scraps. Learned how the booze she left around can make the pain go away. Had me quite a habit by the age of nine. Mom mostly ignored me. Only got off her ass and enrolled me in school to get me out of her hair. I was glad to get away from that shit hole but never did good in school and never made friends. None of them wanted to know the dirty kid in crappy clothes. And a geek I met later told me... See this face?" She raised a hand to her cheek.

"What about it?"

"Notice it's crooked?"

She could tell that they did.

"This geek knew all kinds of science crap. He saw my face and told me that the less symmetrical people are, the less fit they seem for survival and the less attractive that makes 'em. They're ugly." She shrugged. "What would I know? At first, it bothered me that other kids were disgusted by me.

"Then I learned to go into my 'zone', and it stopped hurting."

The men nodded. They had seen her in her safe-zone.

"Somebody turned Mom in to Child Protection and they pulled me out when I was nine. Foster homes then, and more abuse, until I had enough bullshit. Hit the streets at sixteen and paid my way with you-know-what. Thank god for free clinics." She sipped her beer.

Aaron asked, "You finish school?"

"Right," she said wryly. "Graduated with honors from FU. Course not! Gave that up with foster homes. Lot of the street kids went, but I don't know how they handled it. Didn't seem like much of a loss to me."

"You don't use drugs. How'd you miss that?"

"They scared the shit out of me. First thing I saw on the street was a dead kid. Overdosed on heroin. I tried weed, but it made me paranoid. Alcohol worked for me, but you're more likely to get busted walking around with an open container of booze than with a heroin kit in your pocket.

"When I hit twenty one, I cleaned up and found a job."

Patty asked, "How old are you?"

"Twenty three."

"I thought you were older."

"Street life puts the miles on. Hasn't been a picnic since then, either."

Aaron asked, "Why did you leave Des Moines?"

"Give me your hand."

Aaron put his hand in hers, she pressed it up to her head behind her left ear and worked his fingertips through the hair. "Feel that?"

He felt the slight ridge, lying vertically, interrupted regularly with young stitching scars.

"Guy I was living with hit me one time too many. Gave me that scar and the guts to finally get out."

Her audience let their shock show.

"That's it," Phia said. "End of story."

They drank quietly through half a glass of beer, each looking at their own glass and buried in their own thoughts.

"So," Phia said, "If you want me out of the house I can be gone early tomorrow. Tonight if you want."

Aaron looked surprised and said, "God, no. Why would you have to go?"

She cocked her head. "You're a funny guy." But it's what she expected.

That night, after sex for the first time with Aaron since his return, Phia thought back on her internal discussion about disturbing Aaron with too much knowledge. Would it hurt him less to reveal her secret now, or later? She obviously benefited by delaying. But what if she dropped dead before giving Aaron a warning? That would be rotten treatment of the best man she ever knew, a man with whom she might actually fall in love, a man who—she was afraid—could fall in love with her.

What would he do if she came clean? She knew that he would just take her on as a deeper responsibility, and that was the most cruel thing she could do to him, because any effort to save her would fail.

Goddamn, she marveled. I thought life was complicated before.

Daniel Peterson

14. Phia, Nick, Aaron, and Stephanie

The week before Thanksgiving, on one of Phia's nights off, she awoke to the sound of a ringtone and Aaron's sonorous voice answering his phone.

"Yeah?" He listened. "Okay," he said, and pressed "end".

Aaron's feet hit the floor like a rumble of distant thunder.

Phia asked, "What's up?"

"Oh. Steph is back at it."

"Back at what?"

"Drinking. Becky called, worried. I have to go."

"I'll go with you."

"Go to sleep," Aaron said. "It's my problem."

She switched on a light. "No, it isn't. Never has been."

"And it sure isn't yours."

"You're my problem. You might need help. I'm coming."

Aaron did something that Phia had never seen. He slumped in defeat. A small pain stabbed her heart.

On their way out the door, Phia said, "I'll call Nick."

"No. Let him sleep."

"We might need him. Not sure I could carry half of Stephanie."

Aaron grudgingly acceded.

When Phia explained to Nick, he said, "We'll have to take my KIA. Not room in Aaron's truck for four. Swing by my place. I'll be ready."

"Where is she?" Nick asked later when they were backing out of the driveway.

"Becky figured the Topping Bar."

Phia asked, "Is that a franchise? We had one in Des Moines."

"No idea."

Nick cruised the bar parking lot until they located the open slot closest to the door.

Steph was seated at a table with another woman and two men, all expounding in an animated conversation to which none of them listened. Steph's arm was bare of the cast she had worn for so long. Aaron, Nick and Phia walked to the table to stand facing Steph, but it took her a few moments to notice them. She looked up smiling vaguely until she recognized them, then she grinned sarcastically.

"Oh, look," she said, "I's the posse. An' they brough' their li'l piece o' pussy. Ha! The piece o' pussy posse! Say tha' three times fas'."

Her table fellows stopped talking and looked up at the Giffins and Phia.

"Come on, Steph," Aaron said. "Time to go home."

"Wha' for? Place doesn' close for 'n hour."

"You need sleep."

"Li'l tired. Nuttin' a beer won' cure."

"Let's go. We'll get you home safe. Say goodnight to your friends."

"Fuck off," Steph said.

Aaron sighed. He walked around the table, squatted beside her, pulled her left arm over his shoulder and put his right around her waist to help her from the chair, but she tried to wiggle out of his grip.

"Why don't you let her stay?" One of the men with her said. "She's havin' fun."

Nick said, "This kind of fun will kill her. Almost did already."

The drunk man who had spoken looked up-and-down and side-to-side at the Giffins and did not return to Steph's defense.

When Aaron pulled Steph tighter to him and lifted hard, she shrieked and yelled, "Rape! Rape!"

Two bouncers came over so Aaron set Steph down.

"Listen," he said to them, "this is my wife and she needs to get home."

"No!" Steph yelled. "Divorcin' 'im. He beats me!"

Aaron looked at the ceiling and sighed, "Oh, Steph."

"That's not true," he told the bouncers. "She's drunk."

"Sorry, dude," one of the bouncers said. "Don't know what your home life is like, don't care, but we can't let you bother the customers. You can sit and have a drink, or you can go."

Aaron said, "She needs to get out of here."

"Not if she don't want to."

Phia could see that Aaron was getting angry—even-tempered Aaron! She stepped up between him and them, and said to the bouncers, "You know, there are three ways we can handle this. One, you can call a cab and put her in it. Which might be a rotten trick on the cabbie. Two, you can let us walk her out. Three, we can call the police to help remove her for her own safety. In that case, I suppose there'll be a citation against the bar because you obviously should have stopped serving her two hours ago. What do you want to do?"

Steph shouted, "Slap the li'l bitch!"

The bouncers looked at each other, stepped away to consult between themselves, then returned. One said, "We'll help you get her as far as the door, but only after you let me see your ID. And I'll be taking your license plate number, too."

Aaron pulled his wallet, removed his drivers license and handed it to the man, who brought out his phone and snapped a picture, checked the photo for clarity, then handed the license back.

"You chicken-shit bastards," Steph berated the bouncers.

But, even in her state, she knew that her battle was lost, and didn't resist this time when Aaron helped her stand. They danced the drunk waltz getting her to the door and the car. They loaded her while one of the bouncers took a picture of Nick's front license plate.

At Becky's house, Aaron held his key chain out to Phia,

dangling from the key which he still had for the front door. Nick helped Aaron slide the nearly comatose Stephanie out of the car and walk her into the house. As they entered, the far bedroom light came on, then Becky appeared, flipping on the hallway light.

"You found her. Good," Becky said.

Phia looked around the house and shivered, remembering the last time she was here. There stood the woman whom Phia almost shot in her own bed. That would have been bad luck. Very bad luck. It would have been Phia's old type of luck, her pre-Moscow type of luck, where everything she did went sour, and doing nothing gave an equally bad result.

They were sidling Stephanie along the hall toward her bedroom when she muttered something.

"What?" Aaron asked.

"Gotta pee."

Becky said, "Better get her on the toilet."

The others waited outside while Aaron helped her balance and keep from passing out. This time she did not object to his presence.

"Okay," Aaron called out the door. Stephanie was covered and on her feet.

Nick helped bring her out, down the hall, into the bedroom and onto her bed. Becky, Nick and Phia left to let Aaron get Steph's clothes off, pajamas on, and place her properly for the night, on her stomach, face lying at the edge of the bed. Becky returned with a wastebasket and a big plastic garbage bag to place under the wastebasket in case of spatters or a clear miss.

Back in the living room, Aaron said, "You have a spare blanket, Becky? I'll bed down on the couch in case she needs anything."

"I can watch her."

"You have work tomorrow. I don't." He frowned. That wasn't true. He wondered if Steph was just doing this to make sure the house failed.

"Okay." Becky went looking for the blanket.

To Nick and Phia, Aaron said, "You two go home."

"Phia, I'll call tomorrow when I can leave, if you'll come get me. And thanks for taking care of the bouncers. I was ready to do something stupid."

She felt sorry for his frustration with the whole, pointless mess. "Glad I could help. I'll come when you call," she said. "Anything you need."

"Okay. Thanks. G'night."

They wished him luck and left as Becky came in with the blanket.

15. Aaron and Steph

Aaron lay awake on the couch the remainder of that miserable night, wondering what he could do to get life back on an even keel—his life, Steph's life, and Nick's. All of their futures were now riding on what he would do in the next few days, days which should be dedicated to the remodel, but which must go to helping Steph. He was not worried about Phia's future, given her independence and mobility. She didn't have to be torn down with the rest. This thought dulled his misery.

It distressed him that Steph could behave in a way which not only harmed her physical health, but also destroyed her own chance at a share of profit from the house. Even finding herself a job was impossible unless she could give up drinking.

The drinking. That came on only after she walked out on him. Before then, she was indifferent to alcohol, seriously drunk maybe twice in all their time together.

Aaron arose once in darkness, around three, to check on her. She was still breathing, so she hadn't drunk enough for alcohol poisoning to kill her, and part of that might be explained by the sour smell and the vomit in and around the wastebasket. He went out, found a new garbage bag, brought it back, slid the used one away from the bed and placed the new one. He rolled up the foul one. In the bathroom he dumped the wastebasket into the toilet, rinsed it, flushed, and carried the wastebasket back to Steph. He took the smelly, rolled garbage bag all the way outside to the trash can. As a last thought, he stepped into the bathroom and sprayed air freshener around, then again in Steph's room.

When Becky came out in the morning, already showered and dressed for her job as a physical therapist, Aaron got up and greeted her. He went down the hall to check Steph again, who was still breathing but still oblivious to the world.

"She okay?" Becky asked when he joined her in the kitchen.

"She'll live." He smiled grimly. "But she won't like it."

"What'll we do?"

Aaron sighed heavily. "Been thinkin' all night. All I can figure is keep her away from the booze till she dries out, then get her a job. Without a job, she'll go back to the bars. If she can't stay out of the bars, this'll happen again, or we'll have to give up. Crappy choices."

Becky nodded. "When I'm here, I can keep her in line. And call you if she's too much."

"I appreciate that. Frees me up to get a little done on the house."

"*The House*. Stephanie really took it bad."

"She tried to explain after the car wreck. I had no idea."

"Want some coffee?"

"Yeah. Can't sleep anyway."

She poured and passed it over. "Here," she said. "A nap in a cup."

He smiled. "Thanks. The worst of it is, we're committed on the house. Have to stick with the plan to come out with anything. And Steph's doing all she can to kill it and throw everything away. Now I get *her* sense of frustration. I see the trap closing on me, but there's nothing I can do."

"It'll turn out."

Aaron laughed darkly. "I told that to Phia and she said things always do turn out. Always bad. Maybe she has a point."

"Who is Phia, anyway?"

What a good question, Aaron thought. More to the point, who is she to me? I told Phia she's too scary. We have almost nothing in common. Our histories are night and day to each other.

Still, he liked being with her, working with her, playing with her. He felt a small tremor and couldn't say if it was dread or affection, or both.

He said, "Just a hard-luck girl from Iowa. A survivor. She's rough around the edges, but strangely sane considering her past. It made me cringe to hear what she's been through, and I think she didn't tell us everything."

"How did you meet her?"

"Chance. She ran out of cash and needed somebody to get her drunk. We were convenient Idaho rubes."

"And she just moved in?"

"She really knows her rubes."

Becky laughed. "Steph is obsessed with her. Thinks she's a demon in woman skin."

"Steph doesn't have a right to judge. Pot and kettle."

"Steph's a good friend but, yeah, you have a point. Well," she said, standing, "I gotta get to work."

Aaron walked down the hall and stood outside

Stephanie's doorway, studying the sleeping woman. For the briefest moment, he wished that she had died in the night, but was instantly remorseful.

Much later, he heard her stirring and grabbed the Naproxen, the antacids and the water, assembled ahead of need. By the time she was sitting upright, he was at the bedside, offering them to her.

She looked blurrily at the items in his hands, then up at his face. "What the hell you doin' here?"

"We'll talk about it later. Take these."

"Gotta pee."

"Take these first. You'll just pass out if you don't."

Steph weaved as she reached out for the pills, popped them in and swallowed them with the tall glass of water. She paled, but it stayed down.

Aaron asked, "You need help to the bathroom?"

"Think I got it."

She had to brace on every available handhold to get there on her own, but she did. While in the bathroom, she loaded back up with massive amounts of water. She returned to the bed, pulled the covers over her head and descended into blackness.

"We'll talk later," Aaron whispered as he withdrew.

He went to the kitchen and set up the items he would need to quickly assemble a breakfast for Stephanie of oatmeal, toast, a sliced apple and coffee, then he lay down on the couch and finally slept, despite the coffee he drank earlier with Becky.

Stephanie shuffled to the bathroom just after noon, eyes drooping and hair wild. Aaron awoke at the toilet flushing and was on his feet by the time she dragged herself to the living room. He guided her to a chair at the dining table.

"Sit, wait."

He punched the "on" button of the coffee maker and lit the burner under the waiting oatmeal water. Ten minutes later he was serving her at the table.

"Why you here?" Steph asked again, watching him place the breakfast in front of her. She had already sipped several times at the heavily creamed coffee.

Aaron pulled up the opposite chair and sat. "Is your mind clear enough to have a talk?"

"Not if it's about that house."

"It isn't. It's about you and how we're going to get you back on course."

"Why do you care? Oh!" She smiled wanly. "It *is* about the damn house. I'm slowin' you down and spending your money on daiquiris."

"No, Steph. I hate that you're killing yourself. And I'm going to help whether you want it or not."

"Yeah. Saint Aaron and his latest charity case. Isn't your whore enough to occupy your martyrdom? Oh, that's right, she's '*paying*' her own way. No charity case there."

He wanted to ask when she had become so mean, but didn't. He said, "This is how it'll be. You're going to stay off the booze long enough to break the habit, and then we're going to find you a job. Simple."

"If you think I'll give up my only consoling vice, then *you're* simple."

"It's gonna happen. Has to happen."

"Why? Why can't you just..." She studied him for a minute. "Okay, Saint Aaron. Do your worst. But don't whine when you fail."

"How do you feel right now?"

"Like shit. But I know it doesn't last. And if I get a stiff drink around three o'clock, everything is good again."

Aaron shook his head. "Finish your breakfast. And you need a shower."

She shrugged. But she worked her slow, distasteful way through the food, got up, went into the bathroom and started the water running.

Aaron realized that he also needed a shower, so when Steph finished, he took one himself, dressing back in his worn clothes afterward.

He came out almost refreshed and looked around for Steph. She was gone.

"Shit!"

"Hey," Phia answered her phone. "Ready to come home?"

"No," Aaron said. "But I need my truck."

"What's up?"

"Steph snuck out on me."

Phia paused for a long time and decided not to ask if it was wasted effort going after Stephanie. The soon-to-be ex-wife was not nearly "X" enough in Phia's opinion. It gave the phrase "going after Stephanie" a whole different twist in Phia's mind. She tried to remember where her gun was. Yeah, still in the Geo Metro's glove box. "Okay. Be there soon."

Aaron paced and fumed. Next time, he thought, I'll take her phone. See her grab a taxi then, out here in the shrub-burbs.

Phia had never exercised much empathy in her life, but she understood tit-for-tat, an eye for an eye, and she was bright enough to envision the opposite, a state where somebody could do so little evil to you that you would wish them the same, like the way she felt about Aaron. Of course, it could be that she just never had an opportunity to express empathy within the transient relationships that she knew. Maybe she had always known empathy and only repressed it until now, when she found a worthy subject. She remembered the pain she felt when she watched the cloud of defeat surround Aaron. Now she must decide what she could do about his pain.

"Want me to come with you?" Phia asked as Aaron crossed from her car to his truck.

"No. But thanks."

"What if you run into some bouncers?"

He smiled. "Can I give them your phone number?"

"I'll expect their call."

Aaron waved to her and climbed into his truck.

He shut the engine off in the front parking lot of the Topping Bar. Pulling his phone out, he called Steph but she refused to answer. He didn't want to drop in cold like last night, figuring that if he was gentler, and with her in a more grounded state, Steph might be persuaded without hysterics to come home and finish sobering up. Aaron texted her, "Wher r U?"

"Happy."

"Am outside."

"Unhappy?"

"The bar."

"Am not there."

"Not where?" Aaron climbed out of the truck and started toward the front door, then felt a premonition.

"Not at Topping," Steph texted.

Aaron walked to the corner of the building and caught sight of her just disappearing around the back corner of the bar. She had walked out the side door, trying to avoid him.

He laughed, then walked back across the front wall of the bar, stopping just short of the last corner which she must come around to complete her circuit. As she stealthily approached, he heard the crunch of gravel under her foot and flattened himself tight against the wall. Steph stopped, leaned cautiously out to look around the corner and found Aaron's face inches away.

"Shit!" she yipped, jumping back. "Don't do that!"

Aaron smiled at her. "Steph, doesn't this behavior give you a hint?"

"What behavior?"

"Sneaking around. Sneaking out of your house, sneaking out of the bar. You're in too deep."

"I don't need you telling me how to run my life."

"For god sake, it's two in the afternoon. Come on. Let's get you home."

She glared lightning bolts at him for a moment, then her shoulders slumped. She walked toward his truck with him following.

At Becky's house, Aaron brewed another pot of strong coffee and pulled up a streaming video series. The rest of the afternoon they watched three episodes, until Becky came home.

Before leaving, Aaron took Becky aside and told her about Steph bolting earlier, and their scintillating time since. "So keep an eye on her, and call if you need me."

Becky nodded, said, "Thanks," and went back to start her shift with Steph.

Six days into drying out, Steph's withdrawal hit critical. She had to have a drink. Becky called Aaron at seven that evening.

"I couldn't stop her," Becky said. "She was raving and pleading and wouldn't let me touch her."

"Where'd she go?"

"I don't know. She ran outside, walked down the street phoning a cab."

"Okay, thanks. I'll look around."

Aaron told Nick what was up and headed toward the door. Nick rolled his eyes.

Aaron started at the Topping Bar. There was no point in trying to call or text her this time. He knew she would not risk contact again. A careful walk-through didn't turn her up, so he caught a woman leaving the restroom, described Steph and asked if she was inside.

She assessed him. "No, but if you're not set on that

particular woman, there are spares at my table. Come have a drink."

It struck Aaron as funny that women who would not have given him a second thought in high school now considered him acceptable.

He smiled. "Thanks, but I'll pass."

"The girls will be crushed," the woman said, smiling and turning away.

The Mountain View Bar enjoyed a bigger crowd, so it took more time to make sure that Steph was not there. The woman he stopped outside the restroom was unfriendly this time.

"No. Get away."

Aaron apologized and waited for a less spiky woman, who, when she finally came out, confirmed that Steph was not in there.

Aaron was repeating the process at The Fleidermaus when his phone chirped.

"Hey, Phia. What's up?"

"Stephanie's here."

"At Huevos?"

"Yeah."

"Okay, thanks. Be right over."

Stephanie sat alone in a booth awaiting service, cringing at the noise level in Huevos with each outburst of fans watching the semi-final football game on multiple screens. But she decided to live with it, because she knew that Aaron would never look for her in a sports bar. She loathed sports. Where was that server?

Finally, a figure appeared at her shoulder with a pad and pen.

"At last," Steph said, looking up.

Their eyes met and both said, "You."

Steph continued, "No wonder service is so crappy here."

Phia glared. "You..." she started.

"Me?" Steph smirked.

"You've been against me from before you even met me. I never did anything to you. You act like I took your man. I didn't. You threw him away."

"And he didn't even bounce before you cushioned his landing."

"No. When you insulted me at the house, there was nothing between me and Aaron. Nothing! You were all over me like stink on shit when I was just a house guest."

"I want a beer. Isn't that your job?"

"How about a glass of water and a sandwich?"

"Beer. IPA." When Phia didn't write the order, or move, or stop glaring, Steph said, "Aaron never mentioned you had a job. I'm impressed that you're an employed, contributing member of society. I had no idea they run a prostitution ring here."

Phia restrained herself, sliding into her safe zone instead of stabbing Steph in the throat with her pen. Steph watched internal darkness absorb Phia's rage, and twinged. Phia scrawled the order deeply into her pad and strode away.

Phia took a quick break, pulling out her phone while waiting for the orders to be filled by the bartender. She called Aaron.

Steph's was the last order she delivered. Before she set the drink down, she slid into the booth facing Steph and said, "I'll give you your damn drink, on me, if you'll let me talk and keep your mouth shut."

Stephanie looked at the beer, thought about tackling the bitch and taking it away. Another ear-splitting yell filled the bar. But the little monster scared her. Small as she was, Phia radiated danger.

"Okay. Have your say." She held out her hand.

Phia passed the beer across.

"You want to blame everybody else for your misery. You focus on me because I'm handy to blame for losing your husband. But it was you. Did you think the lawsuit was the way to get him back?"

Steph squeezed in, "That was the lawyer. Men have always run my life..."

"Men have run your life?! Men like Aaron, trying to *save* your life? Men like a proud father? High school jocks worshiping you? When have you been 'run' by a man? Try having a full-grown man stick a dry finger in you when you're seven. Try living with a foster father who fucks you in the ass when his wife is out. Won't get pregnant! Try living on the street without sucking up to the worst asshole you can find because you know that at least he'll keep you for himself. Hang onto him, do everything he wants. Everything! Just so he won't kick you out for the hyenas." She paused to calm herself. "Men haven't run your life."

Steph stuttered, "I... I..."

Quieter, since even some of the nearby sports fans had heard, Phia said, "How about a guy who makes you do a porn vid online, or a chicken-shit, meth monster that beats you up 'cause he feels like it? Men have run your life? You don't know how easy you had it. Grow up!"

Steph sat with her hand around the full glass of beer, staring at Phia.

"Now," Phia said, "drink your damn beer and go to Hell."

Aaron walked up. The unexpected scene of these two women facing each other in a booth baffled and scared him.

Steph looked up at Aaron. She looked back at Phia, pushed the beer toward her and said, "No. You have it."

"Aaron," she said, looking up. "Can you give me a ride home?"

Aaron wondered what had happened between the two women, but was afraid to ask.

Daniel Peterson

16. Phia, Aaron and Nick

They settled into the new routine. Aaron left in the morning to take his shift with Stephanie before Phia got out of bed. Phia cleaned up remodel mess in the day and performed her assigned tasks. She left for work, the Giffins returned shortly after, ate the meal Phia made for them and labored at remodel through the evening. Nick left, Aaron bedded down, Phia returned from work late at night and snuggled in.

Phia suffered too much time alone, too much time to think. The idea of finishing off Stephanie danced through her mind, but now with less urgency because of two conditions. First, since the twenty-four hour watch had begun on Stephanie, there was less opportunity to reach her. And second, Phia had reassessed how the Giffins would feel about her getting rid of Steph. Before, the benefit to them was worth spending her short, remaining span in jail. And Aaron's emotional commitment to Phia then was tenuous enough that, at worst, he would feel he'd unknowingly taken a snake into his home, and good riddance. But now, he was attached to her. Even in her emotionally crippled state, she could see that. She suspected that Aaron was very nearly in love with her—would be if not for the distraction from Steph. While Phia fell in love with him at the same time, so she could no longer betray him by harming Steph.

She searched again for means to repay their kindness beyond the tiny rent she paid. The rent was intentionally small so she could rebuild her bank account quickly with the idea that she could need it again soon, when she continued traveling toward the sunset. But what was the point in that? Her urgency for leaving came from the desire to get away from the Giffins before she died, or before she must tell Aaron that she would be dropping dead on him. If she just waited for the aneurysm to blow, or gathered the nerve to tell them, then she might not have to move on, in which case there was no reason to rebuild her account. She could pump every dollar of her earnings into the house. The pay at her job was not great, but on game nights at the Huevos Sports Bar, she made good tips.

On her next day off, sitting down to supper with the brothers, Phia said, "Giffins, I have a proposition."

"Oh?" Aaron said.

"I want to be a partner in the business."

The boys did their standard glance at each other.

Aaron said, "We can't let you. We don't want to drag you down, too, if things fall apart."

"That's my decision, isn't it?"

"I suppose, but..."

"No. No but. You think you have to take care of me, but I'm a grown woman, and can live my own life. I want to be a respected business-woman."

Nick laughed, hooking his thumbs in the suspenders of his worn, dirty overalls. "Yeah, you'd be right up there at the top with us."

"Exactly," she said. "Right where I want to be."

The boys took a bite of their food, a sip from their glasses and thought, while Phia chewed and watched them.

Nick said, "What'd you have in mind?"

"Not a full partnership. A share for the money I can put

up between now and the sale. Of course," she smiled, "I could live here rent free."

The men laughed. "Obviously," Aaron said. "How much you think you can swing?"

"Everything, except two hundred or so to chip in on food, buy pit-stop, and keep my phone."

"Too much," Nick said.

"Not if I get it back when we sell. Living here is cheap."

They ate for awhile.

Aaron looked in Nick's eyes. Nick made a small shrug. "Okay," Aaron said, "I'll call the lawyer tomorrow."

Phia hoisted her water glass. "Here's to us, partners!" she toasted.

"Partners," they responded.

Daniel Peterson

17. Aaron and Steph

Aaron stopped his truck at the curb, walked to the door and met Becky as she came out to leave for work.

"Good luck," Becky said.

"Thanks. I'm hoping."

Inside, he said, "Morning, Steph" as he passed by her into the kitchen to pour himself a cup of coffee. He joined her at the dining table and asked, "About ready?"

She was dressed in her best business clothes, looking perky after three weeks without a drink. The withdrawal had been hell, but the brain-chemistry swings finally flattened out, leaving her as well as before the blow-up. She had a nine o'clock appointment for a job interview as a bookkeeper at a retail irrigation supply outlet.

"Ready as I'll ever be. Let's go."

Aaron slugged back a swallow of hot coffee, set the cup down and stood, grimacing. "Wow!" he said. "Hot! Who needs caffeine when you have pain?"

Before she left the cab of the truck, Aaron leaned over and kissed her on the cheek. "Knock 'em dead."

She smiled. "Thanks."

He watched her walk to the building, thinking how attractive she still was. It was too bad she had burned the bridge between them, and left the hollow in his life which was filled more and more by the enigmatic little Phia.

Even given Phia's autobiography, there were untapped depths in her which he might never access. But the mysteries did not make her less appealing, and he was falling for her. It was hard to imagine a future without her, especially since formalizing the new partnership.

He switched the radio on at low volume, twisted in the seat to semi-recline and covered his eyes with his cap, trying to rest for whatever came next.

The passenger door opened. Aaron slid back his cap and sat up. Steph was smiling. He raised his brows.

"I got it. Start Monday." She climbed into the cab.

"All right! Congrats!" He leaned over, wrapped his arm around her for a side hug, and went in for another kiss on her cheek. She turned her face and met his lips with hers. Surprised, Aaron held the kiss anyway, then pushed away. "Sorry," he said.

"I'm not. You put up with a lot. You stuck with me. Thanks."

He shrugged. "Glad I could help. Let's take you home." He fired up the engine.

Aaron parked at Becky's house. Stephanie climbed from the cab and looked back at him when he didn't.

"You're not coming in?"

"No. You have the stability you wanted. You can go it alone."

"I won't mind if you come in. It would be nice."

She was looking at him with a suggestive smile, an old, familiar expression of desire. But those days were gone. The kiss in the truck did not repair the gulf between them, and he was looking forward to his life becoming less complicated, not more.

"I'm sorry, Steph," he said gently. "I can't. You'll be fine. You're smart, talented, beautiful, everything going for you. You deserve better than me."

Her face fell, then turned sour. "That Ph..." she started bitterly, but stopped and relaxed. "Sorry. I know it's my own fault. If Phia hadn't stepped in, somebody else would." She smiled. "Though that somebody else might not have been Satan's daughter."

Aaron smiled back. "Should I swing by in the morning and drive you to work?"

"No. Beck and I have it worked out. She'll drop me off on the way to her job. I can share expenses until I get my own car. But I'll call you if she can't do it."

"Good. And good luck."

She smiled forlornly, closed the truck door, gave a small wave and Aaron drove away.

Daniel Peterson

18. Phia and Aaron

Phia was laying out old newspapers to catch spatters from priming the pre-cut trim and sills, lying across sawhorses, for the master bedroom windows. She and Aaron had moved downstairs while they reworked the upstairs bedrooms. Except for the spiders, Phia was just as glad to be with him there. She glanced at the print on the entertainment page of the paper as she spread it and shouted, "Hey!"

Aaron came out of the bedroom where he was putting on the last coat of paint.

"What?"

"Christine and the Queens is playing at the Bing in Spokane tomorrow night. Isn't it time for a break? Let's go."

"Who?"

"French singer. Amazing voice, cool style. Strange dancer." She assessed her man (a new, delightful awareness for her—her man) and smiled. "You will love 'er."

"Okay, a break's good" Aaron said. "But it's a long drive. Leave in the afternoon and get back early morning next day."

"Hold on," Phia said, pulling out her phone.

After ten minutes she said, "The Hotel Ruby is just across the street. We can book there and come home the next day. All rested. Ready to install trim. Nick will barely miss us."

Aaron looked thoughtful, then shrugged. "Why not?"

They ate dinner at the Europa, walking distance from the hotel, came back to spruce up a little, have a drink in the Sapphire Lounge, and crossed the street to the theater.

As they left the performance, they were both exclaiming, Aaron about Christine and the Queens, and Phia about the theater itself.

"That," Phia repeated, "is the most gorgeous theater I have ever seen."

Aaron said, "Wait till you see the Woldson Fox, up the street." He squeezed her hand. "Thanks for suggesting this."

They drank a nightcap at the Sapphire, went upstairs and bedded down, though sleep was delayed by other activity. Then they both slept deeply and well.

Through the next day's drive home, they were quiet and introspective. Aaron, not talkative at the best of times, was stone silent. Beside Aaron, the usually loquacious Phia, with a small smile, reveled in the evening's afterglow and the company of her stolid man. She thought about the items she had once rejected from her bucket list as unattainable, first among them genuine love. Now, as far as she could tell, she was living that. Having kids was still not an option, of course; even if she survived pregnancy, childbirth would almost certainly burst the aneurysm, killing her to leave the child motherless. But, if the child would live, what better father could it have than Aaron?

She restarted her bucket list from the reverse view of those items she had already achieved. It would make checking off items easier. Fall into mutual, real love. Done. Become a carpenter. Well on the way to being checked off. Become a successful business-woman. Give that a half check; the successful part might take more time than she could expect.

As they neared the Moscow city limit, her smile grew, she looked up at Aaron, reached out and took his right hand from where it rested inside his thigh, squeezing it.

"Giffin." she said. "I have to be with you."

"You are."

"Not just now. For the rest of my life. I need to be with you. Don't ever send me away."

Aaron blushed as he squeezed her hand in return and stuttered, "I... I've been trying to figure a way to say the same thing."

Phia pulled his hand up to press against her cheek, then kissed the back of it, and placed it on her knee, to rest there until they got home.

The following Monday, Phia told Aaron she had some personal business around town and left him to work alone. She drove to the office of the lawyer who represented the Giffins.

She was forced to wait fifty minutes before entry, since she didn't have an appointment, and the first thing she asked, before sitting, was, "Everything I say here is secret, right?"

"Yes," Maxwell Ruben, said. "Please sit. How can I help?"

"I need a will."

Ruben raised his brows. "It's never too early make a will, but unusual for someone so young." He flattened his expression. "What do you have in mind?"

"You don't want to know why?"

"Unless it's a legal matter, it's outside my scope. I'm curious, but that's not pertinent. What do you need?"

"Simple. Everything I have goes to Aaron and Nick Giffin."

"And what does 'everything' entail?"

"Not much yet. Some savings, my junker car. But my share of the partnership will grow. It all goes to them."

"Are you married?"

"No. Why?"

"A spouse is given significant claim as primary inheritor. Since you're not married, that doesn't apply. We can do what you want. I'll draw it up and you can come in next week to sign. The receptionist will give you an appointment."

"Do the boys have to know they're in my will?"

"It's not customary."

"Thanks, Mr. Ruben. See you next week."

She stood and let herself out. The receptionist double-checked the address and phone number which they already had on file for Phia, and calculated a small billing invoice which Phia paid with her debit card.

That same day, the last reason Phia could have for killing Stephanie evaporated. The divorce was signed, formalized and recorded. Among the provisions of the divorce, Steph would receive a part of the profit from the house proportional to one half of the resources which came from her and Aaron's funds before the divorce. They evenly split the remainder of their common savings account.

Even if Steph died mysteriously now, there would be no economic gain for the Giffins, nor, Phia realized, for herself, the new partner. Unless Steph cooked up some further misery to dump upon Aaron, she was safe from the homicidal schemes of little Phia. Adding to Steph's safety was that Phia was no longer merely a grateful tenant of the Giffin brothers, willing to throw away her remaining days. She now looked forward to extending her life with Aaron, to milk it for every moment of joy.

Phia dug through her car's glove box, under the gun and ammunition, until she found the old prescriptions given to her by Dr. Genoa. She stopped at a pharmacy. It took an ungodly long time to have them filled because the prescription date was so old, and the physician was unknown to the pharmacist. The pharmacist's assistant phoned Des Moines at the number on the prescription. Dr. Genoa was not available, but the receptionist offered to text him immediately. Phia sat impatiently for twenty minutes, then got up and poked around in the aisles looking at canes with colorful butterflies printed on them, and braces for backs and knees and elbows and ankles and necks. She sat in the automated blood pressure checker and took her reading. One-twenty-six over seventy-one. The pharmacist called her to the window.

"Here you go, Ms. Marshall. And Dr. Genoa asked me to give you this number and have you call him."

Phia looked curiously at the number. Was it customary for a doctor to invite calls from a patient? "You know what it's about?"

"He said he has information about your mother."

"My mother? I don't get it."

"That's all he said."

"Okay. Thanks. How much for the pills?" She tucked

the phone number into her wallet.

19. Family Christmas

Phia found that minor scrapes and cuts took longer to stop bleeding because of the anticoagulant, and the blood pressure medicine caused occasional faintness when she stood up suddenly. She ignored these.

Aaron, watching her stand, noticed the pause as she waited for her vision and balance to return.

"You okay?" He asked.

"Fine. Just pregnant."

His jaw dropped. "What?!" He imagined faulty condoms and a failed contraceptive implant, wondered if it was his, and finally arrived at the question of what having an infant around the house would do to the project.

Phia watched the traumatic expressions flicker across his face until she couldn't stand to see him suffer. She laughed out loud, grabbing his face in her hands. "I'm joking!" she said. "Poor boy. Relax!"

Surprise shaped his face, followed by anger, and then relief. "That was mean," he said.

"I'm sorry. It was. But the look on your face! I wish I'd been ready with a camera. You don't want to start a family?"

"Not something I planned. At least not yet." He shook his head and smiled. "And don't do that to me again."

"Okay. No family yet, no jokes about babies." She hugged him. "I'm really sorry," she said in his ear. But she was not sorry that it had distracted him from asking about her faintness.

When they broke apart, Aaron said, "Speaking of family, my folks invited us up for Christmas dinner."

Phia paled. "Oh, shit! Meeting the parents. Never had to do that before." She paused, looked at him wryly. "Or is this bullshit to get back for my joke?"

"It's for real. Don't worry. They'll love you."

"You tell them about us?"

"No. They'd think it's too soon after Stephanie. As far as they're concerned, you're just our new business partner, brought in to fill the money gap. They'll suspect more. Be patient with 'em."

"Guess I'll be sleeping *alone* on the couch."

"'Fraid so. But it's in Dad's man cave, and it folds out to a comfortable bed."

"Room for two?"

He smiled. "I will not be sneaking in. And I won't tell you where my room is."

"Now who's being mean? We the only ones going?"

"Our sister will be there with her family. And Nick and Patty."

"How long we staying?"

"Two nights. Drive up Christmas Eve and come home day after Christmas."

Phia liked to hear Aaron calling this place their home. It warmed her heart, so she hugged him again. Since the day when they acknowledged their feelings, she had occupied a soft, euphoric haze. Or maybe that was just low blood pressure.

She found Dr. Genoa's phone number in her wallet while paying for groceries, almost rolling it into a wad and throwing it on the floor. But she tucked it back away. How could he even know her mother, and tie the two of them together, and *what* about her mother? Should Phia care? That afternoon, leaving for work, she paused in the driveway, pulled out the little slip of paper and entered the number into her phone. She reluctantly pressed call.

"Hello? Who is this?" Dr. Genoa asked.

"Phia Marshall. You wanted me to call?"

"Oh! Phia! Thanks for getting back to me. I've been trying to locate you for three weeks. You're hard to find."

"That's how I like it. What's up?"

"A couple of things. First, and more urgently, your mother is very ill. She's under hospice care in a nursing home. And seems to have nobody to be with her."

"No surprise there. So what?"

"But... I thought you'd want to be here."

"Why?"

The doctor hesitated. "Do you understand what hospice care is?"

"Intensive care for really sick people?"

"It's end-of-life care."

She paused. "As in, she's dying?"

"Yes."

Phia held the phone quietly for a moment. "Ain't we all," she said. "From what?"

"Lung cancer."

"Yeah. She smoked like a chimney."

"She asks about you. Can I have the staff tell her that you'll be coming?"

"No. I gotta think about this."

Genoa said, "I don't understand."

"If you knew my mother and the shit I lived with, you'd understand."

"She must have somebody else, then? She wasn't an orphan was she?"

"She has a sister somewhere. They haven't talked in ten years. She has two uncles, but they don't have anything to do with her since grandma died. No idea how to contact any of 'em."

He digested this. "You should make up your mind soon. I doubt she has two months."

"Question, Doc. How did you put this together? I haven't seen her in two years."

"When she came in, she talked about her daughter, Phia. Her nurse remembered you and mentioned the coincidence to me. How many Phias could there be? So I looked in records under your mother's last name, Marshall, and there you were."

"Okay, Doc. Thanks for letting me know. I'll be in touch."

"Wait, there's more."

"Still here."

"After you left the hospital, I did some searching. There is a new technique in clinical trials right now that might fix your aneurysm. If you qualify, treatment is free."

A huge, scary void opened in Phia's core, threatening to swallow her and turn her inside out. She breathed heavily while the doctor waited. "Don't do this," she said.

"Do what? I thought you'd welcome good news."

"Don't. Don't give me hope. Good things don't happen to me. The timing here is just too perfect. Right now I'm happier than I ever been, and making me hope just scares the shit out of me. It'll all be jinxed." She retreated to her safe zone. Dully, she said, "I don't have a right to hope."

"Phia, that's not true. If your life is better now, that proves you do have the right. It happened, it's possible, it can happen again."

"Doc. Don't."

"Okay. But I assume this unexpected happiness involves another person. Maybe you should discuss it with him."

Phia surfaced from her state enough to think about her gentle, innocent lover and about his inevitable pain, whatever happened next. The doc had a point. Maybe Aaron should have some choice in the matter. That would be reason for her to think carefully before discarding this ridiculous hope.

Merle and Esther Giffin, the parents, lived in Hayden in the house they built when the children were in their teens. Esther's parents died years before, but Merle's were still alive, in their late seventies, presently at a snow-bird RV park in Yuma, Arizona where they spent winters. Merle and Esther's twenty-seven year old daughter, Celestia, lived in Seattle with her husband, Appeditis MacKay, and their daughter, Daphne.

Aaron and Phia left Moscow at four in the afternoon. Snow started falling a half hour up the road, but did not accumulate at a rate to create serious hazard. Aaron slowed to accommodate the flurry and to extend this private time together.

At the front door of the Giffin home, Aaron rapped twice and pushed it open. The parents sat in front of the television watching a traditional, infinitely repeated Christmas special. A real tree stood in the corner exuding coniferous scent, lit and covered in decorations that Aaron remembered from childhood.

The parents turned. "There they are," Esther called.

Merle turned off the TV and they stood to receive introduction.

Aaron said, "Phia, this is the folks."

"Call us Merle and Esther," Esther said.

Aaron continued, "Folks, this is Phia Marshall, the new business partner."

Phia shook their hands and Esther hugged her. Phia held out a colorfully wrapped gift for Esther. "This is for you, Mrs..., uh, Esther."

"Oh, son," Esther said. "Didn't you tell her we don't exchange gifts among the adults?"

"I did, but Phia has a mind of her own. Here, Phia, let me take your coat." He hung their coats in the closet beside the front door.

Another double knock sounded. Nick and Patty entered. Greetings were repeated all around and Nick hung up coats.

"Everybody sit," Esther said, gesturing to the arrayed

furniture. "Anybody want something to drink? Coffee, tea, cocoa, eggnog, beer, wine?"

The Giffins all looked expectantly at Phia.

"That cocoa sounds good," Phia said.

"Eggnog," Merle said.

"Same," Aaron said.

"Wine?" Patty asked.

Nick said, "Let me help, Mom."

The two of them went to the kitchen as the rest selected seating. Before they returned with the drinks, they heard chatter of extra voices from the living room as Celestia's family arrived. Nick leaned out through the kitchen arch and called, "Hi, all! Drinks?"

"Eggnog for adults, cocoa for Daph," his sister answered.

"How was the drive?" Merle asked his son-in-law.

"Snoqualmie was compacted snow, but not bad. Radio said more snow came in about an hour after we made it over. The trip home might be hairy."

Aaron said, "S'posed to clear up, so they should have it plowed. 'Course, there could be avalanches."

Esther and Nick came out with two trays of drinks and passed them around, then joined the conversation.

The parents and sister focused on the new partner, watching closely and attending her words. They knew about Aaron's divorce, so they were seeking a clue that he was back in the game. Aaron's face remained neutral and unreadable. Phia was nervous under scrutiny and occasionally looked at one or the other of the boys for reassurance, but gave no sign of attachment. She became uncomfortable and deflecting about her past, so the topic was dropped. The Giffin parents and Celestia were dubious about the boys taking Phia as a partner on such short acquaintance, and unsatisfied by the glossed-over story of their meeting, but they held their tongues.

To take heat off of Phia without giving up pursuit, Esther asked Aaron, "How's Steph doing? And how are you holding up?"

"Pretty good. Both of us." He resisted a glance at Phia. "Becky says Steph's getting to work every day and there's no sign of booze. And I'm happy for her. Steph said she just needed something more stable than speculating on a remodeled house. She was right."

"Speaking of which," Merle asked, "that about done?"

Nick shook his head. Aaron said, "No. Way behind. I hoped we'd be done by Christmas, and start the next house. But with Stephanie's settlement, we won't profit on this first place. Won't make a living wage. In January, I'll look for a part time job. With three incomes, we can swing a down payment by June. If the house sells before then, even better."

Merle said, "Do you..."

"No!" Aaron and Nick said simultaneously. Aaron finished, "We don't need a loan. Thanks, Dad."

"Had to ask." Merle smiled.

Nick said, "Foreclosed houses come up every week. One will fit, and it'll all click."

Phia blushed, unnoticed by the others, when she thought about how her problems could postpone or jam up the click.

Christmas day began with coffee and cocoa, and presents opened by four year old Daphne, then a very light breakfast in anticipation of the main event later. The conversation from Christmas Eve continued, but more relaxed, so Phia loosened up and dropped her guard. She glanced fondly at Aaron when she thought nobody was watching. But somebody is always watching.

Over Christmas dinner, Celestia harassed Aaron about his divorce. "You drive away women better than you drive a wheelbarrow. You need to be more like Dad."

Aaron grumbled, and Nick said, "The problem is that Stephanie should be more like Mom."

Esther laughed. "You've insulted both me and your father in one swipe."

Nick became flustered and Merle snorted.

"No," Merle said, "they know where they get their stubborn streak. And so do I. As for you, old woman, you're a saint."

Celestia said to her brothers, "Then Aaron should have chosen more wisely."

"I learned from my mistake," Aaron said blandly.

Phia kept her head down, eating.

After the meal, everybody packed their dinnerware into the kitchen, stacking it by the sink. Nick stayed in the kitchen with the ladies to help clean up while Daphne returned to the living room with the remaining three men.

"Who you sucking up to?" Phia asked Nick.

Nick looked sheepish and Esther said, "He's always been

willing to help me with the 'woman's work' since he was little."

Phia said, "Is it still called that? Woman's work?" She barely restrained a terse remark about the only exclusive woman's work being birthing and nursing babies, but she remembered her status as a guest. She turned away, grabbed a wet dishcloth and said, "I'll wipe the table." She wished she had a big cigar to light up and take to sit among the privileged class and their penises and testicles.

That evening, Esther and Nick were working drinks duty, like the night before, when Celestia came into the kitchen and said, "Mom, let Nick and me handle the drinks. You did more than enough with that amazing dinner. Go."

Esther peered dubiously at her children, then nodded and said, "I could stand to get off my feet."

As soon as Esther was out of the room Celestia whispered to Nick, "We need to talk."

"Don't whisper. It makes me nervous."

"Out on the sun porch," she whispered.

He looked at the enclosed, unheated back porch, then at his sister. She nodded vigorously. He shrugged and they stepped out the door.

She said, "Does Aaron know that Phia's in love with him?"

"Is that our concern?"

"Watch the way Phia looks at him. She's more than just a business partner."

Nick sighed. "I'm pretty sure it's a mutual thing." He shrugged. "They're adults."

Celestia shook her head. "Love and business don't mix. There'll be trouble. For you, too."

He frowned. "Let's just be happy for them." He thought he knew their business partner pretty well, despite hazy patches in her story, and felt that she would not harm the business or, especially, Aaron. "Don't worry about it."

"Somebody has to. You should."

"It'll be fine."

"But..."

Nick shook his head and went back in to finish their chore.

They transported the drinks and joined the others in the living room. Through the evening, Celestia kept her eye on both Phia and Aaron. Phia tossed discrete, warm looks toward Aaron and, once, Celestia saw Aaron return a soft smile. So it was true. She hoped the effect on the boys' business would not be disastrous. And she hoped that Aaron was not jumping the gun, starting a new relationship so soon after Stephanie, and with somebody about whom so little was known. Except that she must have good taste in men. Was that enough?

Phia woke to the light clash of dishes being stacked away, and a burbling coffee dripper. Her bedroom was the only one on the main floor, and she was not sleeping well in the strange bed without Aaron. She picked up her cell phone. The time read four-fifteen. Sleep wouldn't likely come again, so she rolled out of bed and tossed on clothes. Coffee would be good.

Celestia was emptying the draining rack and the dishwasher when Phia said, "Good morning."

Celestia jumped.

Phia said, "Sorry, didn't mean to scare you."

"That's okay. Just didn't know anybody else was up. Sorry if I woke you."

"No, I been up and down all night. You're up early."

"We have to start for Seattle by nine, and I didn't want to leave the kitchen for Mom."

"Let me help. Just tell me where stuff goes."

After working together for a while Celestia said, "You like Aaron."

Phia let this sink in and said, "Guess I wasn't hiding it very well."

Celestia smiled. "Can't blame you, he's a good man."

"You won't get an argument. Best man I ever met."

"You got together pretty quick."

Phia shrugged. "It just sort of happened."

"I'm curious what made it happen. Why him? That pan goes under the counter in the corner."

Phia inserted the pan in a stack. "He's generous."

"That's the last pan. You want coffee?"

"Love one."

Celestia pulled two cups back out of the cupboard, filled them and set them on the breakfast bar. "Cream? Sugar?"

Phia shook her head and climbed onto a stool.

Celestia said, "He got that from Dad. The generosity. Growing up, I thought that's how everybody was. When I was twelve, we took a camping vacation around the Southwest. We were on a desert road in southern Utah, miles from nowhere. Came on an old International Scout pulled over with its hood up and steaming. Naturally, Dad stopped. Couple of young women were looking at the engine. Their radiator was low, the engine got hot, so they shut it off. Dad got a couple water jugs out of our trunk and told them to start their rig so he could refill the radiator. It wouldn't crank. Dad found a broken wire and fixed that. Then he turned our car around, pulled up close and jump-started the Scout. While it was charging, he refilled their radiator. Mom pulled two more gallons of water out of the trunk and gave them to the women. As we were loading to leave, they thanked us over and over for stopping. Dad said there was no need for thanks; this desert was not the kind of place you could drive by somebody in trouble without stopping. One of the women said two cars had already passed. So I learned not everybody is like Dad."

Phia said, "Other way 'round for me. Thought nobody was generous. Aaron showed me different. And it wasn't just the way he treated *me*. We took a get-away to Spokane. On the way home he drove the back roads to show me some of the country. One gravel road was straight and smooth so we were clipping along good, spraying gravel and throwing up a ton of dust when we saw a guy coming on a bicycle. As we got close, Aaron slowed down to a crawl. When we got right to the guy, he gave us a big grin and waved like crazy. Everybody but Aaron had dusted him. I asked Aaron what made him think to slow down, and he said it didn't occur to him to *not* slow down."

"That's the thing. It's built in."

"Did you know he apologizes to a bug if he has to kill it?"

"What...?"

Esther and Merle walked into the kitchen.

"Well!" Esther said. "What are you two doing up so early?"

Celestia said, "Just comparing notes about your oldest child. Want coffee?"

Celestia's family packed for the drive home and everybody gathered by the front door to wish them a good trip. Phia was discomfited when little Daphne hugged her thigh, but she knelt and hugged Daphne properly in return. Phia was not accustomed to small children.

When she hugged Phia goodbye, Celestia whispered in her ear, "Be good to my brothers."

Phia answered sincerely, "There is nobody in the world I would rather be good to."

As their hug parted, Celestia looked down into Phia's face. Celestia smiled at her and nodded. They could become friends, she thought. "You and I are going to be good friends," she said.

Phia and Aaron left later, but early enough for Phia to get to work on time. Her enlightening inclusion to a loving family Christmas occupied Phia's mind on the drive. Among other things, it explained why the Giffin boys were who they were. Aaron noticed her silence but did not press, knowing that if it was pertinent, she would speak.

Aaron was slowing the truck, entering the small town of Tensed. Phia silently read the name on the city-limit sign, which she still mispronounced even after he had corrected her, then she blurted, "My mother's dying."

He glanced over. "Sorry to hear that. Kind of sudden?"

"I just found out. And don't feel too sorry. She's always been a waste of skin."

Aaron didn't know how to respond.

"It's true." Phia said. "Your family, though. Good people. You like each other. To me that's just weird. And when everything else goes to hell, there they are. I'm thinking, maybe even my worthless mother needs family now."

"So," Aaron said, "you want to be with her."

"No, I don't *want* to, but maybe it would be good for the old witch. And help my karma."

"Go. We'll manage."

"You sure?"

"Yup. This will be your only chance to say goodbye. And you'll kick yourself the rest of your life if you don't."

Phia thought, the rest of my short, short life.

"Okay. I'll pack when we get home and hit the road in the morning."

Aaron said, "Fly. Driving might get you there too late."

"Can't. My..." She stopped.

"Your what?"

"I have a condition. Flying gives me a screaming headache."

Aaron thought it unlikely she had ever flown to discover her "condition", so this was an excuse to cover a fear of flying, but it was her choice.

At work that evening Phia told her manager about needing time off to see her dying mother. The manager was sympathetic, but had heard this excuse before. Phia didn't try to convince him. Regardless of his sympathy, the best he could do was offer her the next job opening after her return. He couldn't operate short handed; New Year's Eve was next week. And he couldn't dump somebody after she returned, somebody who had applied in good faith.

"Sure," Phia said. "I get it. I'll check in when I get back. Thanks."

"Do that. Next spot we have, you get first shot. Good luck with your mother."

Aaron kissed her goodbye in the morning and said, "Call if you need anything. I can grab a plane and meet you there."

"Thanks. But I can handle it. And you need to focus on the house."

"I know. Drive safe. Call when you hit the motel."

"And you be good. No cheap women and wild parties."

Aaron said with mock sincerity, "How about expensive women and mild parties?"

She raised a small fist. "How about a broken nose?"

20. Phia

Phia retraced, in reverse, the trip of last summer that brought her out of Hell and into her little paradise on earth. She could have made it in three days, but I-80 was closed by a blizzard in Nebraska, forcing her to hole up in a crowded, decrepit, smelly motel for two nights.

Boredom set in around noon of the stalled day. She bundled up and went for a walk, pulling the hood of her winter coat tight against the blowing snow. There was not much to see here at the best of times, but even that was hidden by drifting snow. Her mood reflected the environment and she wondered if it derived from the environment, or just happened to emulate it, or whether her mood was what created the dismal weather. She knew for sure that both she and the weather were dismal. She had her fill of it after twenty minutes and turned around. Her path back took her past a small grocery, nearly devoid of customers, where she paused to buy snacks and a six-pack of Guinness.

A bored businessman pouring himself a cup of coffee in the motel lobby tried to start a conversation as she paused to throw back her hood and stomp snow from her boots.

"Some weather," he said.

She looked at him with suspicion and breezed by, up the stairs and into the corridor to her room. He followed her up the steps and watched down the hall to see where she stopped. As she opened the door he called, "Would you like a coffee? It'll warm you up."

Phia glanced at him dully, pushed into the room, closed the door, and locked it. She leaned forward to look through the spy hole. In the distorted view she watched the man hesitate, turn and go back down.

Phia set her grocery bag on the table, went back and checked the spy hole again. She let herself out into the unoccupied hallway. She walked to the stairs at the far end, away from the lobby, peering down the steps before proceeding down two flights and out the door to the parking lot. She unlocked her car's passenger door, opened it and dug through the glove box for her pistol and ammunition. Slipping them into her coat pocket, she re-locked the car, and returned to her room.

Phia checked that the gun's magazine was full, though she did not expect to need the pistol for the bored businessman. He didn't seem the type to make trouble, but the motel was over-full, and in any group that size at least one would be a predator. Unusual circumstances, like an unexpected delay in a strange town, can unleash whatever light, social bonds hold a predator in check.

She was surprised at herself. In the pre-Aaron days, she would have sat in her room, forgetting the gun, awaiting whatever happened, willing to make it hard on whoever came at her but complacent, hopeless. Now, damn it, she was not going to roll with any more punches. She was going to punch.

The television played an old, black and white, Swedish movie, dubbed in English, and she was working on her second Guinness, when a light knock rapped at the door. She picked up her pistol, released the safety, chambered a round, and watched the movie. The knock did not come again. There were no more interruptions that day.

The movie ended, leaving her puzzled—something about a guy trying to escape Death by beating Death at chess.

But Death cheats. Phia didn't know how to play chess. Maybe Death would go for a game of seven card stud; she knew a few tricks of her own in poker. She muted the television to make her nightly call to her lover.

The next morning the freeway opened so she loaded the car. The last thing she did before pulling out was pop the magazine from her pistol, eject the round from the chamber, and put it back in the magazine. She was glad she hadn't left it in Moscow.

She called Aaron every evening, which cheered her up. After the call she lay on the bed tormented by dreadful, imagined scenarios of what awaited her in Des Moines. During a rest stop on her first travel day, she had called Dr. Genoa to let him tell her mother that Phia was coming. She called again after the delay to adjust her arrival time.

The nearer Phia came to Des Moines, the deeper her dread became, and the deeper her depression—not just a melancholic mood for curling up to a hot cocoa and her favorite sentimental movie, but a real gut-ripper that made her fingers twitch the steering wheel toward every giant, passing freight truck. To combat these feelings, she thought of her new life in Idaho, the greeting she would get on her return, and that maybe, maybe, she would get a chance to extend her life and stay happy for a long time. Oh, that's just stupid, she thought. So she stopped the crazy, hopeful crap and dwelt on Aaron and the Idaho house, however briefly she could enjoy them.

She found a Starbucks with wi-fi, ordered a coffee and searched for motels. Though she had lived on the street, and in her car, and would be capable of either again, she believed it was time to graduate to the comfort of a heated room. It took a long time. Eventually she found a youth hostel at only twenty dollars a night for a bunk-bed in a communal, mixed-gender room, and access to the kitchen and dining room. It was not close to the hospital, but there was a nearby bus-stop.

Phia knew her mother's age only because her birth date was on Phia's birth certificate, the certificate she worked so hard to acquire to get a job as a bar server. The worthless bitch was forty-nine years old. That seemed awfully young for the deathbed, even to twenty-three year old Phia.

Phia thought she made a mistake about which room Antaneek Marshall was in when she peered cautiously through the open door at the four beds and the four occupants—a bunch of withered, old women. Then one of them wheezed, "Phia."

If this shriveled shell-of-a-woman was anybody else but her own mother, Phia's heart would be broken to look at her. But nobody gets over twenty years of resentment in a moment.

"Hey, Ant. How you doin'?" She asked as she walked to the side of the bed, dragging along a nearby chair.

Antaneek shook her head, gasping, "Bad. Food here...is shit. Comes through...this tube..." she gestured feebly at a skinny tube carrying opaque, light blue fluid which led down from a suspended bag and disappeared under the covers, "Skips stomach. Goes straight...to shit." She laughed a couple of weak wheezes. It took her time to speak again. "Shit in...shit out."

It occurred to Phia that this pretty much summarized her mother's life. And her own.

"No wonder you look like shit," Phia said. "I thought maybe that was the cancer."

"Cancer. They say. Bullshit. Bad cold. One

good...thing here. This tube. Morphine. Cheap bastards...give me...button, but...won't give me...full...throttle."

Phia smirked. "We all know if you had 'full throttle' you'd be out of sight by now."

"'S true." Antaneek closed her weary eyes. Phia thought she was asleep. She didn't know what to do. Should she let her mother sleep and come back later? Should she wait until the witch woke up?

"Best thing," Antaneek said, opening her eyes. "Couple of...men nurses...hot for...me."

Phia sighed, shaking her head. "Cool. Men." She thought this was an adequate segue, so she said, "My life's been crazy. Weird, kinda good..."

"But," her mother interrupted, "nobody comes...when I push...call button. Not even...them."

Phia stared at her mother without commiseration. She asked, "You know I'm living in Idaho?"

"When they do...I already pissed...the bed."

"That's a shame, Ant. How's the food?"

Maybe that was cruel.

"Shit! See this...tube?"

Phia found refuge in her evening calls to her man, but being in Des Moines grew harder every day. Clinging for one hour to his voice didn't sustain her for the next twenty-three. When Aaron answered his phone on the sixth day, she was near weeping. She hadn't cried in twelve years.

"Hey," he said. "I can be there in a day. Don't suffer

alone if you don't have to."

She sniffled. She blew her nose. "This..." she said. "I been through some rough shit, but this is horrible. There she lies, just getting more tired, and not dying, and not dying, and not dying. Her breathing gets worse and worse, so I can barely breathe myself. And I miss you *so* much! And she's the same, self-centered bitch."

"I'll come," Aaron said.

She hiccuped. "No. I'll make it. You work on the house. Find a job yet?"

"Not yet." He did not tell her that he wasn't looking, and didn't plan to until she was home.

Phia was sitting with her sleeping mother, watching a video on her phone, when Dr. Genoa came into the room. She was startled to recognize somebody here, and pulled out the earbuds.

"Hello, Phia," he said. "How have you been?"

"I...I'm fine, Doc. How are you? You checkin' on Mom?"

"No, she's not my patient. But you are. I called the nursing home and they said you were here."

"You do house calls?"

"No. Don't want to be drummed out of the corps." He chuckled. "But I do have patients here and thought I would combine duties. How do you feel?"

"Like shit, but it's about this." She gestured at her mother. "Not my time bomb." She pointed at her head.

"Have you talked to your 'important person' about treating your aneurysm?"

"No." She hunched in on herself. "I still don't know if it would be better if he never finds out."

"That's your decision, but sharing can help. I need your signature. Then I can submit you as a candidate for the trials, and release your records. Where are you living?"

"Northern Idaho."

"Okay. There's a team in Seattle that can do the surgery. You can get to Seattle?"

"No problem. Wait! I haven't agreed."

"Here." He pulled out a form. "Sign here, here, and here." He held out a pen.

"Bullshit! I haven't made up my mind."

Genoa frowned. "Phia, all this does is apply for a position in the program. There's a long process before you'll even know if you qualify. But it has to begin now."

"I can back out if I want?"

"Right up to the moment they start anesthesia."

"Okay," she said. She took the pen and signed.

"Good. And fill out your residential and mailing addresses."

Phia hated giving anybody this information, but it was necessary if she decided to take this chance. She wrote down the address of the Giffin house, and the postal box she rented when she got her job.

Genoa stood. "You take care. I'll get this started, and we'll be in touch."

After the doctor left, Antaneek, awakened near the end of the conversation, coughed weakly and said, "You sick?"

Phia looked at her glumly. "Yeah. Not as sick as you, though."

Her mother wheezed out a laugh. "Ain't life...a bitch."

Phia mumbled, "Yeah. You'd know."

Two days later Phia took a break from her dying mother while the woman slept. She used the time to do some grocery shopping for the supper she would fix that evening at the hostel. When she returned to her mother's room there was a woman sitting in Phia's chair, talking quietly and stiffly with Antaneek.

Phia walked up and said, "Hi. Who are you?"

The woman, short like Phia but too thin, professional looking, nicely dressed, about fifty years old, looked up at her. "You must be Phia," she said. "I'm your aunt Denise. Nice to see you again, all grown up." She held out her hand.

Phia ignored the hand. "Mom's sister."

She nodded, retracting her hand. "I just heard." She gestured toward Antaneek.

Antaneek said, "Came from...South...Carolina...to see me."

Denise said, "Can only be here two days."

Phia wasn't sure she liked this abrupt woman any better than her own mother. Where was she during all of those crappy years? "Why the hurry?" Phia asked. "Some kids nibbling on your gingerbread house?"

Denise made a brittle smile. "Could be. I'm a

supervising engineer at Savannah River Site. Office politics never rest."

"You never been here before. Why now?"

Denise frowned. "You're wrong. I came back seven times in twelve years, when you weren't around. Now? I figured I should say goodbye to Ant. It's the only thing left that I can do for her, whether she wants it or not. She never let me help. Never wanted to make something better for the two of you. A waste." She looked back sadly at Antaneek and shook her head.

Phia absorbed this with growing horror. "You mean," she asked, "that Mom had a chance to climb out of that shit hole and wouldn't take it?"

Her aunt looked at her without expression.

"Phia, babe," Antaneek wheezed. "Wasn't that...easy. Just leave? Start new? At what?"

Pressure exploded in Phia. She shrieked, "At anything! You stupid bitch! Why would you not...and leave me...Gah! Let me outta here!" She turned and ran from the nursing home.

Phia entered the hostel, intending to pack and go home to Idaho. She was deeply depressed. And that knocked the stuffing out of her. She dragged into the bunk room, tossed her groceries into her locker, crawled onto her bed and lay there, staring at the ceiling.

An hour later, she pulled her phone out and called Aaron.

"Hey, kid," he answered, "you're early. How's it going?"

"Awful. I just met my aunt that I haven't seen since I was eight."

"That isn't a good thing?"

"No. Just found out she wanted to help mom out of the shit life she lived, but the stupid bitch wouldn't take it. Left me on the street. Stayed in that hell hole with her men and booze and drugs and cigarettes. God, I hate her. I want to come home."

"And I wish you were here, but..."

"But what?"

"Stay. It's rotten to find out you could have had it better. But it doesn't change anything. Your mother was weak. She let you down. You're strong. You did what she couldn't, and without your aunt's help. Take pride. Forgive your mother. I'm sure she's glad you could do what she didn't."

"The bitch doesn't care. She never asked what I'm doing, and interrupts if I try to tell her."

"People can't always say what they want."

Phia breathed into the phone without speaking.

"You okay?" Aaron asked.

"Yeah. As long as I have you."

"Your mom has you. Stick to it."

"You bastard. You're too nice for my own good."

She waited two days, to make sure that her aunt was gone, before going back to the nursing home. When she went in and sat by her mother's bed, she noticed a small card lying on the nearby stand, with her name, "Phia," neatly hand-printed on it in large letters. She picked it up, turned it over, and read aunt Denise's business card with her private number added, also in neat hand-printing.

Phia sat staring at the card, thinking for a long time before she pulled out her wallet and tucked it inside.

Five days later, Antaneek, battling for every breath, stopped trying to talk. She crept a bizarrely youthful hand toward Phia, who picked it up to hold without thinking, without remorse, without recrimination. They sat like that for two hours before Phia realized that her mother was dead. She marveled that she missed the transition, that there was so little difference before and after. She gently laid her mother's hand on the bed and pushed the call button.

"How would I know?" Phia asked the social worker. "I never had a mother die before."

"Okay, we'll work through the steps together. Did your mother have a preference for final rest?"

"I haven't lived with her since I was nine. No clue."

"Religious preference?"

"No idea. Listen. Isn't there a standard way to handle— what's the word—indigents?"

Distastefully the social worker pulled her hands away from the computer keyboard, crossed her arms and said, "Yes. Is it your wish that we deal with her in that fashion?"

"Please. Am I done now?"

"Just sign this form here." She slid it to Phia and pointed at the line.

Phia signed.

"Now you're done."

Daniel Peterson

21. Junior

Junior was manning one of his more productive sales sites. A lot of his suburban clients stopped here before jumping onto the rush-hour freeway toward home, to pick up a dab for their evening relaxation. Business was brisk.

He finalized a sale. As the client walked away, Junior glanced up at the jockeying vehicles to look for the next customer. He idly watched a shapely young woman leave the convenience store and walk to her car at the fuel pump.

Recognition slapped him. He couldn't believe his eyes; it was that bitch Phia. And still driving that crappy little Metro. Well, he had business with her. It was time for a reckoning.

Junior locked his car and started across the lot.

Daniel Peterson

22. Phia

Returning to the hostel, Phia packed in a frenzy, loaded her car, drove away craving escape from this shitty city, but stopped at a gas station beside the freeway to fuel her car, get some cash at the ATM and load up on the usual travel supplies.

She returned to the car and set her right rump into the driver's seat, placing her bag on the passenger seat. She leaned over to pop the receipts into the glove box and was straightening back up when an approaching man caught her attention through the windshield. "Fucking hell," she said. She was going home, and she did not have the time or patience to put up with more bullshit.

As her old—what should he be called, attempted murderer, abuser, controller—boyfriend, Junior walked toward her car, she leaned again to the glove box, removed her pistol, shaking off fluttering receipts, released the safety, chambered a round and turned just as Junior swung open her unlatched door and grabbed her ankle. Junior started pulling. She pointed the pistol and squeezed the trigger three times, making a set of deafening blasts inside the little car and creating three brief dimples in the belly of Junior's winter jacket.

First, Junior marveled at how she could have kicked him in the belly so hard, then the blasts he heard connected with new signals from torn nerves in his abdomen. He screamed, "She shot me!" He let her ankle go.

Phia did kick him then, to get him away from her car. He staggered back, gripping his belly. She collected herself into the seat, slammed the door, started the engine and jetted away as quickly as the little Geo could go.

Phia shook like a chihuahua in a Minnesota blizzard. In her distress she almost missed the turn for the I-80 ramp, but braked hard and turned sharp to correct her over-shot. At the bottom of the ramp she merged with thick, rush-hour traffic and could find no openings to hasten her escape. Juiced on adrenaline, in shock, almost deaf from the confined gun blasts, she could barely focus on driving.

The speed of the cluster in which she drove began to slow, and she began to panic. If the police already had a road block, or diversion, she was caught, and she really needed to get home to her Giffin. But the flow never stopped completely, and one mile further along she saw that an accident in the east-bound lanes drew the attention of gawkers on her side, just enough to impede traffic.

Beyond the accident, speed picked up, though there were a couple more random slowdowns, and in twenty-five minutes she was twenty miles away from the gas station.

Traffic thinned and no blue, flashing lights glared in her mirror, so Phia started to relax. The shakes eased. She glanced down and saw her pistol still lying on the passenger seat with her grocery bag, so she stuck it back in the glove box. Or should she throw it out the window? No, it cost too much to throw away. With that, her brain shifted back into gear and the first thing she did was mentally kick herself for being a complete, absolute idiot. Of course Junior would be at the gas station, but not just because her crappy luck demanded it. When Junior left her for dead in their kitchen and removed his belongings, her assumption was that he left Des Moines. Stupid. Where could he go? He would not want to start over elsewhere, looking for a new meth supplier, or new buyers for his hash oil. And if he kept up business as usual, he would return to the same old haunts, of which that gas station was one, and she *knew* that. Junior had a friend there who, for an occasional hit of free hash oil, told him where the blank areas in the security cameras were, and when management shifted cameras, and to where. That allowed Junior to market freely at the station. It was one of his several outlets.

Stupid! But her new life in Idaho had put Junior gradually out of mind, and of all the dreadful scenarios she imagined finding back in Des Moines, this was not one.

However, on the up side, she did get to gut-shoot the asshole, just as she fantasized all those months ago while lying in her pooled blood.

The morning newspaper's "In Brief" box included a local story: "A man was shot yesterday at 5:10 pm at the Hasty Gas Stop on I-80. Witnesses say the victim, identified by police as Tucker L. Bryant Jr., 25, was pulling a woman from a car when the woman fired three shots and sped away. Bryant was taken to the hospital and is listed in critical condition. The identity of the suspect is not known. Police are reviewing security video. Undisclosed amounts of methamphetamine and THC oil were found in the victim's car, parked at the scene. Anyone with knowledge of the shooting is asked to call..."

By the time the security video was reviewed and an alert spread for Phia and her Geo Metro, she was well beyond Omaha, driving short on sleep, but not speeding. She was, though, pushing the car's little three cylinder engine harder than she ordinarily would. The first time she pulled off for gasoline, she was preparing to swipe her debit card at the pump when a notion stopped her. The police might have her card data by now. If so, they would know she was here, and they could anticipate where she was going. Phia went in to the clerk to prepay with cash.

The police did not have Phia's debit card data, yet. It took time to evaluate the scene of the shooting, transport the victim for medical care, and get the station manager's permission to see the security video. Then they ran the Geo's license plate and identified Phia, a woman of twenty-three, five feet three inches, appearing of northern European ancestry, residing at two different addresses of record. Then they requested a warrant to access the station's credit/debit card files with the card facilitation company. While they waited for card data, the police sent patrol cars to the addresses given on her driver's license and on her car registration. She had not been at either in the last six months, though neighbors at the more recent address, from the car registration, remembered her.

She finally stopped to sleep at a rest area in western Nebraska. After her mind cleared of adrenaline, but before it became shrouded in exhaustion, Phia considered her options. She thought she should plaster dirt on her license plate and the car. No, anything like that would make it stand out, so she did not alter her car, counting on its ordinariness to fade in among others. Along the same thought, she pulled up in the rest area between two other cars which seemed to be settled for the night. She always parked away from others on her first trip west, but now she took advantage of the invisibility found in a group. Phia fell to sleep wrapped in her winter coat with spare clothes piled around her legs. When the chill bit hard enough to wake her, she started the Geo's engine and ran it until the car warmed, then shut it off and slept again.

Before leaving in the small hours, while returning from the toilets, she noticed with irony that drifting snow and road grime obscured her license plates, just like every other car.

Phia listened to as much news on the radio as she could find, but there was no report about Junior. Of course, if a report mentioned him, she might have missed it for not recognizing the name. She knew his last name, but just thought of him as Junior.

Tucker L. Bryant Jr. found at a very early age that his first name rhymed closely with an unfortunate word, which his classmates used liberally. It took two school years and the abandonment of several friendships, but he finally transformed his name to Junior. Even his teachers came in line. He refused to consider his middle name, Lynn, as an option because he knew that it could be a girl's name. Junior wondered why his father passed along such a problematic name to his son after having grown up with it himself. Just being his usual, asshole self, Junior guessed.

Phia would have noticed mention of a shooting, so the news of one more sleaze-ball drug dealer getting his karma adjusted probably didn't rate mention on the radio a state away.

Phia was back on the road after four hours of sleep, with the sun still below the horizon. Two hours later, it crept up into her rear view mirror and another hour after that her phone chirped with Aaron's ring-tone. Oh, shit! She had not called home last evening, hauling ass out of Iowa.

She gathered herself to answer lightly, "Hey, Lover."

"Hey, Pest. You didn't call."

For a second, in her fragile, exhausted state, she flared with resentment, but then remembered that Aaron's remark was spawned from concern.

"It's been crazy. Sorry."

"What happened?"

"Mom died."

"Oh. Sorry." Aaron, though he expected this, didn't know what more to say.

"There was a lot of crap to do. Dealing with a non-existent estate, picking burial service and all. I was tied up, distracted." Lying, she thought, comes easy. Too easy.

"Get it all settled?"

"Yeah. I'm on my way home. Just hit Wyoming. Be there in two days. Shouldn't talk and drive."

"Be careful. Call tonight."

"Okay, bossy beast. I'll call."

She pressed "end" and almost broke down crying. She fought it, but her vision blurred with tears. She didn't dare pull onto the shoulder of the freeway to recover for fear that a police car would stop to check her. Phia wiped her eyes on the sleeve of her shirt and kept driving.

The call from Aaron made her think of another susceptibility. Her phone could be tracked. Even turned off, the police could petition the phone provider to turn it on and track it. In Cheyenne, she pulled over at the first parking spot off the freeway, pried the back off her phone and removed the battery.

"Track it now," she muttered.

She was getting the hang of this fugitive stuff.

Phia drove around until she found a Walmart where she bought a cheap, throw-away phone and air time. This cost only fifty-five dollars, but she paid in cash and saw that her reserve was dangerously depleted. The pittance left would not buy the gas to get to Moscow, not with the winter-reduced fuel economy. Then there was the gas burned at night, keeping her warm enough to sleep. She would soon have to risk using the debit card. A single cash withdrawal would get her home, and would only give the police a single point on her path. But that point would give them the direction and distance to concentrate their search.

Or.

She thought back on her decision to keep her gun instead of pitching it because the pistol cost too much to throw away. It was worth money.

The new, cheap phone included a rudimentary browser. She searched Cheyenne for pawn shops. The first one she stopped at featured guns, and the proprietor was glad to take her cute little pistol in pawn for a good sum, about a third of what she'd paid. She even found the receipt for it in the glove box. The money would help, but would it get her home?

She took time to lunch on the junk food she bought at the gas station where fate had come to visit Junior, and thought about her position. If she got close enough to home, Aaron could meet her and fetch her the rest of the way. But could she get that far, say Grangeville at the worst, on what she had?

Why did Cheyenne tickle her memory? It was something positive, an uncharacteristically warm memory.

Richard and Ruth. They might loan her some money.

The church was difficult for her to remember. She must have still been in shock at the revelation of her numbered days when she came through last time. The sign out front now read, "Ch rch is missing U". She liked the last one better.

Phia knocked on the door of the residence.

Ruth opened the inner door, peered questioningly through the storm door, hesitated, broke into a smile, swung it open and cried, "Phia!" She stepped out and swaddled the smaller woman in a motherly hug. "Phia, you look great! Things have worked out for you."

Phia shrugged. "It's good to see you, Ruth. How's Richard?"

"Oh, he's Richard. If enthusiasm could save the world, it would be a done deal. Come in. How've you been?"

"Never better. I'm working, and in love."

"Wonderful! Come sit. Want a tea? Coffee?"

"Coffee would be great, thanks."

"Be right back."

Ruth put the pot to perking and returned. "So tell me about this love and the work."

"We're partners in a house remodel/resale business. Living in the place we're working on. It's beautiful. Everything about it."

"I'm so happy to hear that. Richard and I were worried when you left us before. You needed a lot of healing. But it looks like you found the cure."

"More than I deserve." She hesitated. "But I'm stuck again in a situation, and wondered if you could help me."

"What is it?"

"I went to Iowa to be with my mother during her last days. I'm going home now, but running short of cash. I could use a loan."

Ruth frowned. "I'm sorry to hear about your mother."

Phia shrugged. "Not to sound mean," she said, "but she brought it on herself."

Ruth nodded slowly. "Let me get our coffees."

Ruth went into the kitchen, pulled out her phone and called Richard. She summarized the situation for him and asked if he could break away. She nodded at his response, ending the call. With poured coffees, Ruth returned to Phia.

"I called Richard. He wants to see you. Be here in a few minutes. So, where's this house you're remodeling?"

"Moscow, Idaho. Ever been there?"

"No, but I've heard the name, like Russia. What's it like?"

"Take a Currier and Ives print, put in more hills, you got it."

Ruth laughed. "I'm tempted to join you."

"You'd like it. And so would Richard. Lot of good heathens up there."

Ruth chuckled and sipped coffee.

Richard arrived.

Phia stood and tolerated another parental hug. Ruth went to fetch another cup of coffee while the others sat and made pleasantries.

When Ruth returned, Richard asked Phia, "So what would this loan entail?"

"Just enough to guarantee gas for me to get home."

Richard nodded. Phia could see his reluctance. "You understand," he said, "we try to help people at the root of their need, without enabling self-destructive behavior."

Phia laughed. "You think I'm addicted to gasoline?"

Ruth and Richard chuckled. "No," he said, "but a loan of money allows a certain unintended latitude in what the borrower acquires."

"Richard," Phia said, "you should be a politician. You got the words."

"Thank you. I think. But you understand what I'm saying?"

"Yeah. Can't loan without knowing what it goes for. Well, that's cool. It was worth a try. Thanks for the coffee. It's been good to see you again, but I gotta hit the road." She stood up. "And thanks for your help last time. You been great."

"Wait," Richard said.

Phia stopped.

"Would you accept the loan in another form? Like ten gallons of gasoline in cans?"

Phia's face lit. "That would be great! That's all I need."

Richard and Ruth watched for disappointment or deceit in Phia's response.

They smiled. "I'm sorry," Richard said, leaning sideways, pulling out his wallet and leafing through it. "Here's forty dollars. It's easier to carry."

Phia looked puzzled but reached out slowly for the cash, like it was bait in a trap.

Richard said, "We just needed to know it was really your root need. You obviously would have taken the gasoline. Sorry we tested you. We like to help, but we try to be realistic."

Phia smiled crookedly. "Good for you. I knew there was a reason to like you guys. You got sense. I will pay this back."

Richard shrugged. "Whenever you can. Just get home safe and stay happy." He stood and Phia hugged him, and Ruth. They escorted her to the door and, this time, when she drove out of the parking lot, she turned to wave goodbye.

That night, her last away from home, she called her man, who was puzzled by the unknown ID from her throw-away phone. "Dropped mine," she said. "Had to get another." She hated the growing burden of lies, but tomorrow, she decided, she would divulge everything, every lie or secret she held— except how close she came to shooting Becky; that would go to the grave with her.

Phia did not fool herself about her police avoidance tactics; she knew they would only reduce the risk of capture en route, though it would take good luck to not be spotted anyway. The police would know before she arrived in Moscow that it was her destination. There was record of her from three months of debit card use. Atypically, as she saw it, her luck held long enough to get home.

Discovering Phia's address was simple once the police accessed her debit card records. The Moscow police couldn't spare a car to sit and wait at the house for Phia to arrive but a patrol drove by occasionally looking for her Geo.

Daniel Peterson

23. Phia, Aaron and Nick

The exhausted Phia arrived at nine. Nick was still there, winding up a project. Nick and Aaron heard her car door shut and were outside sporting grins, to help her with her bags before she could pull them from the trunk. Before the bags, both men hugged her. Aaron gripped her close and kissed her.

"Giffins," Phia said, "I have missed you *so* much. You have no clue how much."

"I have a clue," Aaron said. "Let's get your bags and sit down with a beer while you tell us about your trip."

"Thank god, a beer."

They dropped Phia's bags just inside the newly finished bedroom and retreated to the dining room. Aaron pulled a bottle of Guinness and two tall Busch cans from the fridge, setting them on the folding table in the dining room, in front of three camping chairs.

"Damn, it's good to be home," Phia sighed after the first sip of beer.

"Good to have you home," Aaron agreed.

"To home," Nick toasted, and they drank.

"But," Phia said, "I have stuff to tell you now, before...you'll see..."

She told them about gut-shooting Junior, and not knowing if he was alive or dead, and about the precautions she took getting home to avoid capture until she could tell them about it in person because she wanted to see them a last time before her world went to hell again.

Aaron said, "So, I guess we should call the cops and let them know you're here and want to turn yourself in."

Phia frowned, but nodded. "First, since I'm telling stuff, I have one more thing, something I been keeping from you." She looked contritely from one brother to the other. "And I'm sorry, but I couldn't think of a way to bring it up. It wasn't your business, then I fell in love with Aaron and it was your business. But I didn't want to hurt anybody."

Nick said, "Come on, Phia. We're adults."

She stoically told about the aneurysm, but started crying when she revealed the potential cure. When the telling finished they paused, then Aaron reached out and took her hand.

Aaron said, "Phia, we will get through this. We'll take care of everything. Whatever the law brings, whatever medical crap comes."

She broke down weeping. It was funny how she never cried at the difficult stuff, the bad childhood, the bad men, the beatings, even the aneurysm, but with these men she cried, not from sorrow, but from relief and gratitude. Aaron slid his chair closer and wrapped his arm over her shoulders.

After her tears subsided, Aaron said, "I s'pose we better call the cops."

Nick looked away and said, "Don't think we'll have to." He nodded at the living room wall where blue and red lights flashed against it.

The police processed Phia into jail without allowing contact with the Giffins. Lacking a warrant, and after several phone calls to Des Moines produced no interest in them, the two men were released. Their request to see Phia was denied.

The next morning Aaron went to his lawyer's office at opening time, insisting that Max Ruben see him now, regardless of what he might have planned. Max liked Aaron (they had occasionally visited over beers at the Fleidermaus), a little less at this interruption but, because he liked him, he agreed to see him.

Aaron filled Max in on the disaster, including the background of Phia's previous life and her relationship to Junior.

Max asked, "What are the charges?"

Aaron removed a paper from his shirt pocket and read, "Discharging a firearm in a public space, reckless endangerment, illegal transportation of a firearm, flight to avoid arrest, and the armed assault upon and attempted murder of Tucker L. Bryant, resulting in grievous bodily injury."

"Phia." Max shook his head. "Unbelievable."

"She says she did it, so she can't plead innocent."

"You're getting ahead of the game. They're just holding her for rendition to Iowa. That'll take days to iron out, weeks. She's far from trial, but make sure she doesn't waive rendition or they'll have her out of here quick. I'll make some calls today. And you need to get a good criminal lawyer in Des Moines."

"Then let's get her out on bail."

"We'll apply, but the charges include flight to avoid arrest. The judge will set it high. Can you swing ten percent of four-hundred-thousand?"

"God no. It's all been sunk in the house. What else can we do?"

"Visit her. Reassure her. From what you tell me about Junior, she has a great self defense argument. She might be found guilty of illegal transportation of a firearm but I'd say the attempted murder and assault won't hold up, and the rest of the charges should be dropped. Tell her that. Make sure she doesn't discuss her actions or the charges with anybody but me."

"So, it's just sit and wait."

"I'll talk to some associates, find out who would fit your needs in Des Moines. Until then, yes. Just keep her hopes up, and wait."

"Okay. Thanks, Max."

"No problem. It's billable hours."

Aaron laughed and shook his head, but he knew that Max was not joking.

Later that morning, Maxwell Ruben got a call from Phia. The local police were facilitating a video interview of Phia by the Des Moines police at one in the afternoon and she needed her lawyer.

Max glanced at his appointment list—nothing he couldn't shuffle. "I'll be there," he told her. "I'll come in at twelve-thirty so you can fill me in first hand. I heard it from Aaron, but I need it from you."

"Thanks, Mr. Ruben."

"Glad to help. See you at twelve-thirty."

At the appointed time, Max requested a meeting with his client and he was shown to the visitor's room, where Phia was led in and seated on the other side of a sturdy Plexiglas window. They lifted the phone handsets and Phia said, "Thanks for coming, Mr. Ruben."

"Call me Max. Now, tell me the whole story, including the assault on you last summer."

"Which one?"

"How many times did he assault you?"

"Maybe five altogether. Three last summer."

Anger pinched Max's face. He shook his head. "Okay. First, tell about the one that put you in the hospital."

She started with Junior walking through the door.

Max asked, "What's the address?"

She told him, he made a note, and her story continued.

"Doctor's name?" He jotted that down. "And he took pictures?"

Just before one o'clock, the guard collected Phia, and Max was guided to the interview room where he was searched before entering to sit beside Phia. The corrections officer accompanied Phia, and a police detective joined them.

A video screen in the end of the room lit with the image of a man and a woman. The Moscow detective looked up and spoke, "All here. Her lawyer is Mr. Maxwell Ruben. I think our recorder is running?"

A disembodied voice said, "Running."

"Okay, Des Moines," the detective said.

"Thank you, detective," the woman on the screen said. "I'm detective Malm. With me is detective Shermer. Our recorder is running." With that, Malm spoke the date and time for the record, gave the case number, and listed the names of all present at both ends.

Malm started, "Mr. Ruben, I will address my questions

directly to your client but you may contribute any time you want.

"Ms. Marshall, did you shoot Tucker L. Bryant Jr. on the date of note?"

Phia looked at Max who leaned close and whispered in her ear.

Phia said, "I decline to answer as allowed by my fifth amendment right to not incriminate myself."

Malm asked, "Are you acquainted with Mr. Bryant?"

Ruben nodded and Phia said, "Yes."

Shermer said, "Bryant claims he never met you before you shot him."

Max held up his hand to stop Phia's answer. Then he said, "My client says they were acquainted."

"In what way?"

Phia said, "We lived together."

"Were you intimately involved?"

"You mean did we have sex?"

"Uh... Yes, a sexual relationship."

"Yeah. Seems stupid, I know. He's such an asshole."

Max frowned at her.

"Where was your residence?"

She supplied the address.

Questioning went on for over an hour, after which the Des Moines detectives thanked everybody and the screen blanked. Among other items, they heard of the near-fatal assault by Junior on Phia, and learned the name of the treating doctor. Ruben also filled in with Phia's declaration about the several previous assaults by Bryant upon Phia which had not been documented. He gave them a short list of witnesses likely to confirm bruising and cuts.

For the next three days, detectives Malm and Shermer investigated. They located the landlord of the house where Phia and Junior had lived together. It was the same address listed on Phia's car registration where officers had already interviewed neighbors to confirm her residence. They went further this time, showing pictures of Bryant and receiving corroboration that he did also live there at the same time. They asked the baggy, semi-retired landlord about Bryant, and the girl, and the disposition of the house last summer.

The landlord jumped right to the point. "That Junior Bryant was a worthless son-of-a-bitch. Left me high and dry, no warning, just up and left. House was trashed."

Shermer asked, "Did you find any sign of a fight? Damage? Blood?"

"Blood? I guess, blood. There was a puddle in the kitchen. Enough to float a tugboat. Hair stuck in it. Took forever to scrape it up and wipe it off. Can't get renters with blood sprayed around."

"You've had experience."

"Just sayin'. People don't want to know about ugly stuff."

"Did it occur to you to report this to the police?"

"Report what? It could have been chicken blood for all I knew."

"With hair in it?"

The landlord shrugged.

"Was there blood anywhere else?"

"Edge of the refrigerator door. Few spots on the floor in front of the fridge. And on the counter."

"Did Mr. Bryant contact you after that?"

"No. If he did I would've sweated another month's rent out of him."

"Did Ms. Marshall contact you?"

"No. Only saw her a couple times before they left. Never after. Pretty little piece."

The detectives looked askance at the old man.

"Hey," he said. "No law against lookin'."

Detectives Malm and Shermer made an appointment with Dr. Genoa, who was anxious to do everything he could to help prove Junior's assault on Phia, though his insistence that Junior did it was only hearsay (he had noted the name in his report). His pictures, however, were dramatic. They showed severe cuts and bruising of the face, and the ugly, still bleeding laceration on the back corner of Phia's head. His notes also described the injuries and referred to the serious concussion from blunt-force trauma to her face and head.

Shermer contacted the police in Cheyenne, who located Phia's pistol and her original Moscow purchase receipt, still at the pawn shop. They sealed these and shipped them to Des Moines. The Des Moines lab confirmed that this pistol had fired the bullets removed from Bryant's abdomen.

The detectives studied the security video of the shooting: In the view from behind the car, Phia is clearly identifiable pumping gas, entering the store, returning and getting into her car. She is not directly visible during what follows, but nobody else could have been in the car pulling the trigger and Phia's left foot and calf are visible outside of the open driver's door. Junior enters the camera frame, approaching Phia's car. He opens her door wider, leans down, grabs her ankle, stands and pulls. Three puffs impact Junior's jacket, he drops her foot, grabs his belly and Phia's released foot hauls back and kicks him where his hands are pressed. She closes the door, there's a pause, and she speeds away.

When they weren't visiting Phia, Nick and Aaron's time went to the remodel. They made simple improvements on the downstairs bathroom and bedroom, and installed new storm doors at front and back.

Aaron still refused to look for a part time job. Until Phia's legal problem was concluded, and until they had some better idea of the medical situation, he wanted to be free to maneuver. Money was tight, but he didn't see an alternative. For the moment, he was leaning on his credit cards. If the need became too dire, he would ask his father for a loan.

Phia was not willing to discuss the medical challenge or anything else, like abrupt death, that the future might hold. And she did not have details to pass along beyond what Dr. Genoa had told her. She just told the Giffins that the medicos would contact her.

The Des Moines detectives entered everything they found into the case file, organized their report, included their own deductions and summary, and submitted the file to the prosecuting attorney's office.

In early February, twelve days after Phia was arrested, the local police received a phone call from the prosecuting attorney's office in Iowa, followed by a verifying e-mail, stating that Phia was not going to be charged, and could be released.

The local detective to whom the call was routed asked why.

"It looks like a clear case of self defense. We can't get a conviction on the evidence."

"Firearm transportation?"

"It would cost more to get her back here than it's worth. She doesn't have a criminal record. She bought the gun legally. And it's politically sensitive. Gun rights supporters would have a seizure if we charged a woman for defending herself. Not the intent of the law."

"What about the victim?"

"He was arrested at discharge from the hospital for dealing drugs. He's short a couple feet of intestine, and a yard longer on smarts. Maybe next time he sees a woman he's been pounding on, he'll run away. He might even stop the pounding. Phia Marshall did everybody a favor."

"Okay, we'll process her out. Thanks."

Phia wanted to surprise Aaron, so she did not call him. She waited to one side in the lobby where he would enter and sign in for his daily visit. He arrived and she walked up behind him as he was stating his business to the duty officer.

She said, "Hey, big man. Give a girl a lift?"

He spun. "Phia! You're out!" He hugged her and lifted her off her feet. He set her down and kissed her. When he backed off, he said, "What happened? How?"

"Self defense, just like Max said. They didn't want to spend the money to get me back there for a trial they would lose anyway." She grabbed his head and pulled his face down for another kiss. "God, I missed that in jail."

"What? No jailhouse romance?"

"None of those women are as pretty as you. Let's go home."

They walked out of the lobby with his arm draped protectively over her shoulders and her hand tucked warmly into his left hip pocket.

Aaron patted that hand and asked, "Jail education? You picking my pocket?"

She smiled up at him. "I'm not *picking* your pocket, I'm *choosing* your pocket."

He patted her hand again.

On the way home, Aaron asked, "Was it bad in jail?"

"You kiddin'? That place is like a four star hotel compared to living in a box, with an ox, on the street."

"You're channeling Dr. Seuss."

"Sorry. No, it wasn't bad at all. Free food, warm, dry. Gave us cards to play games. They even gave me my meds on time."

"Meds?"

"I'm taking a couple of things for the aneurysm."

"We should talk about your medical thing."

"Please, not tonight. Tomorrow."

Aaron frowned, but nodded. "I don't know how you handle knowing you're..." He tapered off.

"How else? Scared shitless now that I have a reason to live. Cheer up. I might die, but at least it won't be in jail."

When they got home, Aaron texted Nick with the news. On his next break, Nick texted back, "Beer pizza Fmaus tonite 6."

Aaron sent back, "We there."

Patty claimed previous engagement so it was just the three of them that evening at the Fleidermaus. As they shared beer, pizza and good company, Nick remarked to Phia, "You should write a book. In twenty-three years you lived a century's worth."

"Twenty-four. I turned twenty-four in jail. February third."

"A double celebration! Happy birthday!"

Aaron said, "And I didn't get you a thing."

Phia disputed, "Yes you did. You gave me a new life. To hell with diamonds."

Aaron raised his glass, "To hell with diamonds!"

"To hell with diamonds!" the others agreed.

That night, exhausted by the emotional strain of the past weeks and the well deserved celebration, Phia and Aaron dragged along the hall to the bedroom. They undressed, climbed in bed and spooned up.

After a time, Phia asked, "You too tired to play?"

"What you have in mind? Cribbage?"

"Something more active."

"Badminton?"

"You can call it that if you want," she said, rolling over to face him and kissing him while her hand caressed his hip.

"Is it safe with the aneurysm?"

"It hasn't blown yet. No reason to think it will tonight. And if it does, what a way to go!"

"For you. Could put me off sex the rest of my life."

"Doesn't matter. After me, other women will just disappoint you."

"True. Shall I serve the birdie?"

"Please do."

While they broke fast the next morning, Phia asked, "What's the schedule today?"

"First thing on your list is call your Des Moines doctor, see if he's heard anything and tell him you'll join the trial. And get details about the procedure."

"You are bossy."

Aaron shrugged. She patted his hand, saying, "I haven't made up my mind to do it."

"Of course you'll do it. I want you around forever."

"You're sweet. But there are two things. One, the old saying, 'Live hard, die young and leave a good looking corpse'. Nobody wants to die old and feeble, and I won't. Two, if I die under the knife, it will *shorten* my life. I'd miss years with you."

"It could be nice getting old and feeble together."

"But I *might* die on the table."

"And," Aaron said, "You might die sitting here at this table, or in a car wreck on the way to Seattle. Nobody has a guaranteed old age. You have a chance for normal. Wouldn't you like to see thirty, or sixty? And stay with me to build the business?"

"Love to. Hope that's what happens."

"You'll do the procedure."

"Maybe. I s'pose. Okay, yeah. But it scares me."

"Hey, you're Superwoman. You can leap two bouncers with a single word. Not afraid of anything."

"Got it backward. I'm afraid of everything. But I'm tired of bullshit. Wasted too much of my life on it."

Aaron said, "But now you're not facing the bullshit alone."

She squeezed his hand.

After they cleaned up the breakfast things, Phia went into their bedroom, closed the door and called Dr. Genoa.

Aaron moved tools and materials out of the living room. All of the house interior was finished except for the living room itself, which had been their workshop. To work on it they were transferring the shop tools into the garage.

Dr. Genoa answered his phone, "Hi, Phia. Hold on." She heard the phone rustle against cloth as he muted it by pressing it to his leg. A mumbled conversation went on for about a minute before the phone slid over rough fabric and his voice returned at full volume.

"Hello, how have you been?"

"Ups and downs. Maybe you heard about Junior."

"I did. Can't think of a man more deserving of a few bullets in the belly, but you didn't hear me say that. I saw a sidebar in the paper this morning saying the police called it self defense. So you're out, free and clear, ready for your next adventure."

"Yeah. Not looking forward to it. But my guy twisted my arm. Have you heard any more about the clinical trial?"

"Yes. You've been provisionally accepted. They'll be contacting you, probably less than a month out, with details. They will want you to go to Seattle for tests and imaging, or get them at your local hospital if it has adequate facilities."

"It's a small town. Don't know. But Spokane is less than two hours away, and they have big hospitals."

"That could work. Wait for their call. After the tests, they'll let you know if you'll be brought into the program."

"They might not take me?"

"It's possible. I'm not sure what conditions have to be met. Probably size of aneurysm, shape, thickness of wall in the aneurysm, location."

"So what's this 'procedure' they're testing?"

"It's a special type of stent."

"A what?"

"Stent. It's a small tube, typically inserted into a narrowed artery to prop it open for better blood flow. In your case, it operates differently. The structure is a reinforced tube of your own stem-cell-cultured arterial cells and collagen. It will be collapsed, inserted through a cannula in your carotid artery, passed into your brain and located so it spans the aneurysm. A small tube attached to the stent draws out the blood inside the aneurysm, binding the arterial wall to the stent. When the bond is secure, two or three days, the tube and control wire will be removed. The cannula will be taken out of the carotid, and you'll be discharged. Followup exams will be scheduled. You might have to stay in Seattle a month."

"Who pays room and board?"

"The medical appliance company is paying for everything involved with the research, including food and housing for you and one support person."

"How long will I be on the table?"

"Less than two hours."

"I've had longer traffic jams."

"Any other questions?"

"No, Doc, thanks. I should have taken notes so I could tell Aaron."

"You've mentioned your guy before. Not another Junior, I assume."

"No, this one's human. And he loves me."

"Just what the doctor ordered. You're sure no more questions?"

"Too much info already, but can I call back?"

"Of course. I want you to have everything you need."

"Thanks, Doc. I'll let you go."

"Call anytime. And good luck."

Phia rummaged around until she located a pen and paper, then listed everything she could recall. She set the note on the nightstand and went to help Aaron.

She mused while trudging tools, about how her life was changed in the past months—going from dull, grinding drudgery, to informed despair, to doomed happiness, to a discouraging stint in jail, to hopeful happiness. She might really have a chance to break her jinx and live a real life, a more-or-less normal life.

That night after supper, Phia retrieved the notes to consult while telling the Giffins what she had learned.

Aaron said, "Sounds pretty clear. Nick, I hate to say it, but it looks like you get elected again to stay home and work while I go with Phia."

"Or you could get a job and I could quit." Nick was half serious, but he smiled. "No, you're right. The system ain't broke, let's not fix it. And Patty would kill me."

The next morning, Aaron and Phia started ripping sheet rock off the inside of the exterior wall in the living room. He kept an eye on her and if it looked like she was exerting herself he would step in.

After the third time, she confronted him. "Hey. I never blew my brain out before you knew. I won't now. Back off."

"You don't know that. Stick to the light stuff."

"It's my brain. I'll do what I want."

"I have an interest in your brain. I have some say."

She flared. "You don't have..." She stopped. "We're having our first fight."

"You left the gun in Cheyenne, right?"

"Aaron!" She stepped in and hugged him. "I could never hurt you."

"Okay," he murmured in her ear, "don't hurt me. Let me handle the heavy stuff."

"You are bossy. Okay. You do the heavy crap."

"Thank you. I don't say it enough, but you know I love you."

She kissed him. "I know. It amazes me, but I know."

24. Junior

Some people are destined to be driven by impulse instead of rational thought. Junior did not know he was one of these people, all he knew was that he had to do what he had to do. He was pretty sure he'd heard John Wayne say that. If anybody asked him the reason, he would have claimed honor, which anybody who knew him would call bullshit, because he didn't have an honorable bone in his body. What he saw as honor, others called reputation. He possessed a reputation for meeting business obligations. And he had a reputation for payback if he felt somebody unjustly, or even justly, misused him. There was no greater misuse in his life than being gut-shot by that worthless slut whom he should have hit enough harder that she would be burning in Hell now instead of haunting his revenge-filled fantasies.

The whole time that he lay in the hospital, fighting peritonitis and knitting his bowels back together, Junior plotted.

Two days after his hospital discharge he was standing beside an indifferent public defender, in front of a judge, charged with drug manufacture, possession and trafficking. The prosecutor had toyed with the idea of adding a charge of attempted kidnapping, but the young woman was now in Idaho and the security camera record was not enough to prove intent. Junior's worthless lawyer barely got the bail reduced, but Junior didn't care, as long as he got out. The lawyer called a bail bondsman.

The next morning, Junior bailed out of jail under admonishment to stay in town and report any change in address.

The desk officer recommended avoiding felonious activities and the bail bondsman reinforced this.

When that devil-woman shot him, the police seized Junior's car, along with the drugs in it, and the cash on him. They froze his bank account on the assumption that the funds in it were illegally gained, which was, of course, true. That truth didn't ameliorate his frustration at finding himself momentarily penniless. Perhaps worse, they also seized his phone to track his transactions over the past months. Unfortunately for the police, his supplier and client lists were heavily encrypted, but he didn't have a backup, making a quick return to business difficult. He would have to claw his way back from scratch. Almost.

He borrowed the bondsman's phone to call his mother from the jail lobby.

"Mom, yeah...Fine, great...Yeah...You still have that old phone I gave you? Can you look up Jolly's number and read it to me?...Sure, plug it in...Right, right." He wrote it down. "Okay, Mom. I'll be by later. I need that phone back. Keep it on the charger. See ya." He had given his old phone to her, but his mother still preferred her land line, so she threw his into a desk drawer. Later she bought a new, state-of-the-art cell phone which she only used when she left the house. For once, Junior was glad his mother refused to drag herself out of the last century; her land line was the only phone number which he had committed to memory.

Junior called Jolly to come pick him up, handed the phone back to the bondsman and thanked him. Junior rarely thanked anybody for anything, but pissing off the guy holding his bond seemed stupid even to him.

Jolly took Junior to his mother's house to pick up his partially charged cell phone, which he reintegrated with his phone account. Junior said a perfunctory goodbye to his mother, promised, just like a million times before, to come visit, and left.

Jolly pulled up at Junior's house. "Come on in for a beer, Jolly," Junior said.

"One, then I gotta get home."

"But you can take me to a car dealer on the way, right?"

"Sure."

Junior pulled two beers from the fridge and left Jolly sitting in the living room drinking one while he roamed the house checking his hiding places.

The police used dogs, so all of his drugs, production equipment and paraphernalia were gone, but they only found one of his three stashes of cash. A quick count gave him just under three thousand—a good start.

They finished the beer and Jolly dropped him at a used car lot. "Good luck," Jolly said as Junior shut the door.

A day later, just after noon, Junior was breaking bail, already on the west side of Omaha and traveling just enough over the speed limit that he should not get stopped. He considered getting a gun before he left Des Moines, but rejected the idea for three reasons: He had a felony assault conviction so a background check would screw a legal buy. It would delay his leaving to make the contacts he would need to buy illegally. And he could already feel the thrill of killing the little bitch with his bare hands. He felt sexually aroused just thinking about it.

Court records are a wonderful thing. Unless there is a compelling reason to close a file, they are open to the public. The warrant issued for Phia's arrest included her home address out in Timbuk-idaho. Junior smiled grimly while jotting down the address.

He completed the drive in one, sleepless, meth-fueled marathon and checked in at the most expensive motel in town, but he was too exhausted and hurried to care. He slept for sixteen hours.

25. Phia, Aaron, Nick and Junior

Nick came by before Aaron and Phia got up from bed that morning. He unlocked the door, popped into the house calling, "Just me, loafers. Left my phone here last night. Get up and get to work!"

In that brief span, a car with a temporary Iowa registration in the back window pulled up to park across the street.

"So, she has a boyfriend," Junior muttered as he watched Nick walk from the house, climb into his KIA and leave.

Phia's car sat in the driveway ahead of where the KIA had been, and beside it was an old Dodge pickup.

She's alone, he mused. She might still be in bed.

That was an appetizing thought. He remembered her shapely little body. Double delight—get some dessert before the main course.

Junior sauntered up to the front door as if he owned the place, pretended to unlock it with his car keys and held his breath while he tried the knob. Yes! The idiot boyfriend hadn't bothered to lock it.

He eased it open, slid through and gently pushed it shut behind him, twisting the knob so the latch wouldn't click. As he released the latch, he heard a toilet flush and, turning, he glimpsed an open door down the hall through which he saw a lav and medicine cabinet. In the cabinet mirror he recognized

Phia's nude back, shoulders and head.

Junior stepped quietly to the bathroom door and stood there as Phia turned around. He relished her naked body, and her shock.

"Junior!" she yipped.

"Hi, Phia," he said, smiling. "You have a debt. I'm here to collect."

He stepped toward her, reaching out, but strong hands grabbed the back waistband of his jeans and the collar of his shirt. Junior felt himself levitated backward, through the bathroom door, swung sideways, smashed against the hallway wall. Sheet rock cracked. A fist slammed Junior's side, still tender from surgery. He doubled over and slid to the floor. When he looked up, a big, muscular, naked man loomed there. Junior scrambled backward, crablike, into the living room with the man following. Junior rolled to get his feet under him and came up dipping a hand into his right pocket, fetching out a knife.

The big man stopped. Phia peeked out of the bathroom.

Shit, Junior swore to himself. What the fuck is going on here? Who's this guy if the boyfriend drove away? He couldn't straighten completely, locked in a semi-crouch by the pain in his abdomen. God, I hope I didn't tear something. He also hoped the crouch looked more like a deadly knife-fighting stance than a crippled hunch. The naked guy was at least six feet tall and built like a rock. Junior thought he could take the bastard with the knife if he was in better shape, but right now it hurt too much to try. Better to bluff his way out.

Junior backed through the living room toward the front door, but stopped when he heard it open behind him. He glanced over his shoulder and saw the "boyfriend" who drove away earlier. Shit!

Junior turned so his left side faced the exit and the "boyfriend", held his left palm out toward him, keeping the knife toward the naked guy, and glanced back and forth between them.

Nick stopped in the front door while he assessed the situation.

"Okay," Junior said. "Somebody's gonna get cut if you don't take it easy."

Aaron, puffing like an angry steam engine, said, "Put the knife down and we might let you call the police."

This remark puzzled Junior. Why would he call the police?

The guy behind him clarified. "Instead of just killing you," Nick said.

Junior mustered a sneer. "Who has the knife?"

Phia stepped quietly out of the bathroom, disappearing from Junior's view down the hall. Junior was too involved to do anything about her retreat, but he hoped she didn't come back with that gun. He needed a quick way out of the house, glanced toward the dining room and back exit. That path would pinch him tighter between the brothers. He thought about the closer basement steps behind him, but it might not be an easy exit. Phia returned, still naked, without a gun, stepped up behind Aaron and reached around to hand him a two foot long piece of solid oak handrail.

"Who has a brother standing behind you?" Aaron said as he weighed the club in his hand and then gripped it like a baseball bat.

"If your brother doesn't want his guts on the floor, he'll

back outside." Junior watched the club.

Nick said, "You try to cut me, Aaron will take your head off."

Junior flashed his eyes back and forth. The impasse held for a silent minute, then the naked guy relaxed, smiled and swung his hips left and right, flopping his genitals side to side. Junior could not keep his eyes from glancing down, distracted for a half second.

Aaron was a fair softball player, experienced in games at fire camps, played to fill the time spent on standby. He was a run maker, not known for blasting it out of the park, but for always getting on base and driving others in. He rarely struck out. Junior's knife hand hovered right in the center of Aaron's strike zone. When Junior's gaze dropped, Aaron took the swing.

The knife dented the living room wall and Junior screamed. He folded onto his knees, clutching his shattered, bleeding right hand, then rolled onto his side, pasty white, moaning.

Phia took the club from Aaron and stepped toward Junior, raising it overhead.

"Whoa!" Aaron called and grabbed the club.

Phia glared at Aaron as he pulled it from her hands. She said, "Just a couple good cracks on his head. That's all I ask."

"No. We're not killing anybody."

"It's the only way to handle fucks like this. Otherwise they just keep coming back."

Aaron shook his head.

Junior was barely conscious through the pain and the process of being trussed in tie-down straps from Aaron's truck.

Nick ratcheted the straps tight so Junior could barely twitch. After Junior was secure, Aaron and Phia retreated to the bedroom to dress.

When Junior refocused, his three opponents were parked in camp chairs, sipping coffee and watching him.

Junior grated out through his pain, "You goat-fucking, hick shits. I eat retard shit-eaters like you for breakfast."

Phia said, "Yuck! For breakfast?"

Nick said, "He's awful mouthy for a trussed up hog. Say, Aaron, you nutted the last pig, didn't you? It's my turn."

Aaron frowned dubiously. "Are you sure?"

"Yeah. It was that guy we caught selling meth over by the school."

"By god, you're right. You gonna use a knife or bite 'em off?"

"Well, he doesn't look too clean, and a knife is too quick. Where'd you leave those dull sheep shears?"

Junior was wondering if they would still give him a chance to call the police, when he saw all three look up and out the living room window at flashing blue lights.

"Too late," Aaron said. "The pig got lucky. No castration today. Too bad we don't have another five minutes."

They stood. Phia said, "It don't take me five minutes." She strode to Junior, leaned down and said, "If you ever come back, I will kill you." Then she straightened, gathered her whole, angry strength, raised her foot high and stomped her heel into his testicles. Junior was unconscious when the police entered to save him.

Nick called in sick. They sat around the table trying to unwind, sipping coffee, which didn't help.

Phia asked Nick, "Why'd you come back?"

"Not sure. Just a funny feeling. Got back here and saw the strange car across the street. Spotted Junior through the front window."

"Did you guys really nut a meth dealer?"

Nick shook his head. "No, but Junior didn't know that."

Phia smiled. "I loved the look on his face when Aaron grabbed him and threw him against the wall."

Aaron studied his cup and sighed. "But now I gotta fix the damn sheet rock."

26. Phia and Aaron

The next week Aaron and Phia were applying the second coat of joint compound to the living room wall, and the drywall patch in the hallway, when Phia's phone rang.

She looked at the unidentified caller number.

"Hello?"

"Hi, this is Dr. Montagna at Virginia Mason Hospital in Seattle. Is this Ms. Phia Marshall?"

"Yes."

"Dr. Genoa told you that we would be in touch?"

"Yeah, about the aneurysm."

"Right. Are you still at the same address?"

"Yeah."

"Good. We'll mail you an instruction packet. When you receive it, please call me so we can walk through it together. Any questions?"

"Not yet. Genoa said I need tests."

"That's right. Give me a call after you've read the packet, and we'll schedule them."

"Okay. Thanks."

"Goodbye, Ms. Marshall."

Aaron asked, "That the call?"

"Yup."

"Good. Let's finish this coat and go out for a beer."

"Awful early, ain't it?"

"I don't feel much like work now."

"You're the boss, Bossy. Let's get this mud up and get out of here."

Over the next weeks, they finished the house, put it up for sale, and settled in to wait for Phia's date with the surgeon.

Phia fretted about what was coming—not so much the medical procedure as the idea of finishing her trip to the ocean, or getting close. Moscow had been a sanctuary, safe from her jinx. What would happen outside? What would the end of her road trip bring?

By unspoken agreement, Aaron and Phia lived in the present, and ignored her past and future. They got to know each other better, and grew closer.

They visited the Giffin parents who were fascinated by the story of Junior, the arrest and the exoneration, and by Phia's impending medical challenge.

When the youngsters left, Esther said to Merle, "What do you think of that girl?"

Merle paused to consider. "She's a kick in the pants. And she'll either push him to the top, or send him to Hell."

27. Phia and Aaron

Early on the morning of the third Sunday in May, Phia and Aaron packed.

Phia looked at her pitiful accumulation of clothes. She had brought most of them from Des Moines, and they showed the wear. She felt she should have something nicer for the trip, but that was pointless if she died over there. And pointless if she lived. Why would she need nice clothes? As she folded them, she encountered the faded, threadbare jeans she wore when she crawled, dripping blood, across the hospital parking lot. A permanent stain showed where the vomit had soaked into the fabric. She studied the jeans, uncertain whether to burn them as a reminder of bad times, or to enshrine them as a symbol of the changes that followed. She stuffed them in the bag.

"No funeral," Phia said to Aaron.

"What?"

"When I die, no funeral. Just poke me in a hole and fling dirt on me."

"Why did that come up?"

She simpered and fluttered her eyes. In a southern belle dialect she said, "I simply don't have a *thing* to wear." Then in her normal voice, "And besides, nobody will come."

"And you call me a funny guy." He shook his head and kept packing.

"In fact," she said, "there are burial parks where they

stuff you in a biodegradable bag and bury you near tree roots to slurp up the good from your body. That's what I want."

"Shut up about dying. Pack."

They loaded and left for Seattle in Aaron's truck. Phia sat in her customary spot, the middle of the big bench seat, or, as she called it, thighed-by-thighed, so she could take comfort from Aaron's mass.

They rode among greening wheat fields, and through small, sparse towns, and rabbit brush, and rocky scablands with almost no conversation, listening to the radio for nearly two hours until a set of repetitive, raucous songs got on Aaron's nerves. He switched it off.

"How you doin'?" he asked.

She could not tell him. She couldn't describe the silly fears that built over the recent weeks of waiting. Or say that she had entered a tacit cease-fire, if not truce, with her jinx in Moscow. Or ask what the jinx will do now that she was not only leaving Moscow's influence, but drawing closer to the Pacific ocean and whatever fate was ordained there. She shuddered at the memory of the last time she left Moscow—her disastrous jaunt to Des Moines.

Phia said, "A little down when we left. Better now. Nervous about Seattle. But the rumbly old truck is soothing."

"Need a pee stop?"

"Yeah."

"There's a rest area coming up where we cross three-ninety-five."

After the break and return to the road, Aaron said, "I been curious."

The miles clocked from Moscow were not just antagonizing Phia's jinx. They were also easing Aaron out of their pact of silence. The jigsaw-puzzle past had some missing pieces, the future was upon them, and Aaron wanted to know more.

"About what?"

"Why did you want to be a partner, knowing you didn't have long to live?"

She sighed, shrugged, and said, "Doc Genoa said I might have six years. You guys took me in, I wanted to pay you back. Figured I could help build up the business a little faster. Speed up the remodels by adding some labor. Then drop dead and leave something to show my thanks."

"And a broken heart."

"That was not on purpose. I never expected you to love me. No man ever loved me."

"You must not have met one with any sense."

"It's just as well; they were all losers. If one had said he loved me, I'd have laughed my head off."

"Why did you run west?"

"Following the setting sun. It suited."

"What did you plan when you hit the ocean?"

"A woman in Boise asked me the same thing. I don't know. I considered wading out and never coming back. If nothing else, I wanted to see the ocean, 'cause I never did, and never would if I didn't go now. If not drowned, I probably would have turned north or south and kept right on going."

"So you traded the ocean for Moscow."

"I figured Moscow *was* my ocean, and my sun would set there with you."

"You're a romantic."

"Just sappy."

"Moscow isn't a gateway to the Pacific."

"A detour. I was curious about Idaho."

They drove quietly for five miles.

"What about your list? A bucket list?"

"Yeah, I swapped that for Moscow, too. Started it in Wyoming with stupid stuff. Stuff I never wanted to do before, like climb a mountain, go sailing, play the ukulele. For god sake, play the ukulele! Dying makes you do crazy crap. I scratched off falling in love because I knew it was impossible, even if I lived a hundred years. Then I found you, and a new bucket list filled itself in—learn carpentry, become a business-woman and, right on top, fall in love. Weird world."

"What about sex with two men at once?"

She laughed. "That was never on my list. I just have your word that I said it was; I was too drunk to remember. And too drunk to make sense."

"What about the partnership now that you're not dying? Gonna stick with it, or go learn to sail?"

"We don't know this stent thing will work."

"It'll work. What's your plan?"

"I'm in it for the long haul if you and Nick are. I don't have anything else."

"We didn't know you were dying. It might have made a difference then. Not now."

"Good. I expect to make my first million before thirty."

"Now who's the optimist?"

They drove again immersed only in truck rumble for a time.

Aaron asked, "Why did you have a gun?"

Here it was, the lie she was always going to keep, and she wished she could be honest, but she was not that self-destructive. "It's a mean world, and predators flock to me. Like Junior." To add impact to the lie, she told Aaron about the leering camo-creep in the Burley Walmart parking lot, and the lonely businessman in the Nebraska motel lobby. "Hey!" she said. "I just figured it out! It's what the geek said about my crooked face, and the way lions hunt; I look less fit, so the predators think I'm easy game!"

"What are you talking about?"

"I always wondered why they target me. Thought there was some hidden sign on my forehead. But I'm just limping at the back of the herd, like a sick zebra."

"I'm not sure it works that way with people."

"Of course it does. I'm proof."

Aaron shrugged and dropped it. He didn't have the knowledge or the desire to argue.

Phia did not volunteer *when* she had bought the gun.

"Do you want me to contact your aunt about your medical deal?"

She hesitated. "No," she said. "I feel bad that I thought she disowned mom. Had no idea she offered help. I'm afraid she might feel she owes me now. Not her problem. I'll call her after I heal up and thank her for trying with Mom. Apologize for my crappy attitude last time we met."

Aaron asked, "Do you have a comforting religious belief?"

Phia snorted. "No. I'm relying on you for comfort. God doesn't exist. If He did, He would have stepped in before, so I don't expect Him now."

"Why so sure?"

She patted his thigh. "Will I piss you off?"

"No. I'm like you, just less certain."

"Remember the geek? He also told me about 'pigeon superstition'."

"And that's...?"

"Take a pigeon. Put it in a box with a random, automatic feeder. When food drops out, the pigeon connects whatever it happens to be doing with the food. If it was flapping its wings, it'll try flapping again. Sometimes the flapping coincides with a food drop. It only has to be now-and-then, but the bird believes flapping will bring food, even though it doesn't. Sound familiar? 'Please, God, make uncle John well.' And if by chance uncle John gets better, bingo: God not only exists, He also answers prayers."

"But one religion might be right. It's possible."

"Maybe. A Mexican village has a yearly ritual where 'tiger fighters' battle in the plaza with claw-tipped clubs. They are absolutely convinced that if they don't do this every year, the world will end. They're probably more right than any other religion."

"How's that?"

"Because they've done it every year, and the world hasn't

ended."

Aaron laughed.

In the extending silence, Phia dwelt again on their approach to the coast and what it could mean. She once took comfort in her impending non-existence. Now she deplored it—the idea of not being, of lost awareness, of not knowing Aaron. Her anxiety grew.

She realized she was indulging her own "pigeon superstition", and that she really had no more basis for her fears than for belief in prayer. She appreciated how easily people fall into erroneous, unfounded belief. We're all just pigeons, she thought.

They spoke little until dropping down the west side from Snoqualmie pass, when Aaron said, "Anything you'd like to do in Seattle when you're well enough to go out?"

"Don't know anything about Seattle except the Space Needle."

"Okay, we can do the Space Needle. We can ride the Monorail out. But there's a lot of stuff: Pike Place Market, the underground tour, ferries to the San Juans, window shopping, live theatre, the art museum, a million good restaurants."

"Art museum? You lose Phia somewhere and pick up a hitch hiker? Who you talkin' to?"

"You might like it."

"Put it at the bottom of the list. If we get down that far, I'll give it a try."

"How 'bout we visit my sister while we're here?"

"Sure. I'd like that."

Aaron followed the GPS directions of his cell phone to the heart of Seattle until they saw the hospital sign and, just up from that, the hotel sign. He drove around the block several times until a ten minute parking spot opened.

They unloaded their bags, hefted them around the corner of the Baroness Hotel—an old, brick and concrete, refitted apartment building with antique windows—and into the lobby. The lobby, relative to their experience of cheap motel chains, was strangely luxurious in the fashion of some undefined, mid-twentieth century era. They walked to the reception desk, waited while the clerk finished serving another couple, and stepped up for their turn.

In suite 511, after putting their clothes away and shoving the empty bags into the bottom of the closet, they called Nick. He told about another potential buyer touring the house that afternoon.

"The realtor said they looked pleased."

"Who are they?" Aaron asked.

"Young family, one kid."

"The house would be a good fit."

"I hope that's what they think. How was your drive?"

They chatted, Nick wished them luck and said goodbye.

There was still time and daylight left to explore some of the city, and they needed to stretch their legs after the nearly seven hours in the truck.

They left the hotel and strolled down the hill, hand-in-hand, toward Pike Place Market. When water first came into view between the buildings Phia asked, "Is that the ocean?"

"Sort of. Puget Sound."

She stopped on the sidewalk so Aaron did, too. He turned to see what held her attention. Phia stood with her head cocked, listening. "It must be," she said.

"Must be what?"

"A very Puget Sound; I can barely hear it."

Aaron groaned. "You're not really sane, are you?"

She made a satisfied smile, shrugged and resumed walking, with Aaron chuckling beside her.

She said, "Some day, after the partnership is making a profit, I'd like to see the real thing. The ocean."

But not yet, she thought, don't risk it yet—even this might be too close.

"We'll do that," he said.

The market was entertaining; they got to see the fishmongers throwing fish, and the variety of goods on display awed them.

They window-shopped their way toward Pioneer Square, seeing a gallery displaying artsy wood furniture, a gallery of imaginative carvings and sculptures, a fancy rug seller, and several up-market clothing stores. In their penurious state, they could admire these goods but not buy.

A placard advertised the underground tour, and they determined to come back after Phia's surgery to go through it.

Near the square, Aaron was confronted by a scrawny, fifty-ish panhandler of indeterminate gender, who hugged him. Aaron patted his wallet to confirm it was still there. The panhandler mumbled something about new shoes, so Aaron extracted his wallet and handed over a dollar. The panhandler looked at the bill with disgust and said, "Tha' don' buy shoes. Need shoes!"

"Sorry," Aaron said. "It's all I can spare. Can't afford shoes myself."

"You don' need shoes. Look you feet. Look my feet. Need shoes."

"Really, I'm sorry..."

Phia, standing behind the panhandler, reached up, prepared to duck, and laid her hand on the person's shoulder.

As if clubbed, the panhandler's face went blank, he/she spun out from under the hand and bolted away without even looking at Phia.

Phia shook her head, and Aaron shrugged.

A few blocks later Aaron said. "Hey. Look at the crowd. Notice anything strange?"

She studied the people. "Not particular."

"Think headgear."

She concentrated on the strolling crowds. "Oh! Only street people wear ball caps." Mainstream pedestrians carried umbrellas, wore hooded jackets, or just ignored the rain, but none wore ball caps.

Aaron removed his cap and stuck it in his pocket.

In the room again later, Phia and Aaron looked from the windows of their suite onto the parking lot. On the lot's far side was a continuous, unattractive vista of the back walls of conjoined businesses with faces fronting on the far street. Several of these were eateries bearing large banners, placed for the benefit of hotel residents, advertising the restaurant's name and number.

Aaron and Phia sat tightly together without speaking, she on his lap in the one padded chair in the suite, admiring the view from their high window as the city dimmed from late sun, to twilight, to darkness, when the city itself lit up the sky. Neither moved to turn on interior lights so the room remained shadowed. He was large and she was light; they could have happily stayed like this for hours.

Phia said, "It's been a fun day."

"Yeah," Aaron said. "If this trip wasn't so serious, it would feel like a vacation."

"Kinda cool to get away alone. Like a honeymoon."

Aaron blanched.

Phia couldn't see that in the dim light but said, "Just joking, Giffin. I know you're still bruised."

Quiet descended.

Phia said, "There was good in your marriage. You loved her."

Aaron kept silence.

"Hey," Phia said turning her face to his. "I opened up when you asked. Your turn." To ease the demand she kissed his forehead.

He still hesitated, but started, "We knew each other in high school. Just schoolmates. She was a year behind so not much contact. When there was, we got along, talked some. You say your crooked face is ugly, which it's not, but I didn't do any better with this round mug I got. The jocks got the girls, including Steph. And she was gorgeous. It gave me shakes to sit near her. Didn't make it easy to talk. I learned to control it some and eased my tension every night, hoping..."

Phia guffawed. "Eased your tension?! That's the worst way to say 'jerked off' that I ever heard!"

"Okay, I jerked off every night figuring I'd be more relaxed around her, but it didn't help. Teen boy. Juices flow hard.

"After high school, I went to work for Dad. Steph graduated the next year, went to community college in Spokane. The jocks either went to four year colleges on scholarships or found jobs flipping burgers and got fat. She got her associate's degree in accounting, came home and found a job as a bank teller. Don't know how she didn't get snapped up by some guy in college. She never talked much about it. Sometimes when I cashed my paycheck, there she was. And she was friendlier than in school. Course, she was supposed to be nice to customers, but I thought maybe there was more. Not that it probably mattered but I was looking fit because I was out there every day humping sheet rock and OSB.

"It almost killed me, but I asked her out. She said yes. I had to 'ease my tension' twice that night."

Phia smiled.

"That first date was awful. We went to a movie. A bunch of rude teens three rows back harassed us about the kind of sex we'd have that night and where was her hand right now, and I was supposed to kiss her while I squeezed her tits. She was pissed, said, 'Are you just going to sit there...' And I just sat there. I gave up, too embarrassed to ask for another date. Three months later, cashing my check, she asked me to have coffee with her. It got better from there. Yes, I loved her, and I was happy until I couldn't face the fire lines anymore. Even then I thought the renovation business would fix that and we'd live the rest of our lives together."

"Rough start. Hard end."

"Real hard. If it wasn't for the house and Nick to keep me moving, I would've folded."

"But then you helped her."

"She said I ignored her, killed her dreams. So I figured I owed her."

"Hate to agree with the ex, but I call you bossy for a reason."

His face got hot. "I try to control it."

"I know. And it doesn't matter to me. I want whatever you want. Maybe she never loved you like I do."

"Or she did at first, and didn't after six years of being bossed."

"You would've helped her anyway. It's in you, just like the bossiness. For god sake, I saw you apologize to a spider."

Aaron shrugged, which Phia felt through her arm around his neck. And, she thought, he will help me, too, whether he loves me or not, whether I hurt him or not. But he does love me, and I won't hurt him. Maybe.

She asked, "If I die, will you take her back?"

"You aren't going to die."

"But if I did?"

He paused so long she thought he wouldn't answer. "No," he said. "She seemed willing after we got her dried out, but, like she said, the spark is gone. Maybe if you never came along, I would have considered it. But we'd be right back where we started. Nothing different. We'd break again."

They didn't speak for a while.

They had not eaten supper yet. Phia sighed a long exhale, and this jogged Aaron to glance at the back of the restaurant at the left end of the block and ask, "Do you like Mediterranean food?"

Her head lolled back loosely and rolled away.

"Is that a no?" he asked.

She didn't answer.

"Phia!"

He cradled her head in his hand, bringing it upright to look into her dimly lit, half closed, lifeless eyes.

"Oh, Phia," he moaned. "We were almost there. Two more days. Just two days."

He wept, holding her face against his.

"Okay," he whispered. "No funeral."

28. Aaron

Aaron sat in the small, dark, faux-wood paneled office of the funeral service company. Soft, depressing music sighed out of nowhere and settled on him like soot. The Final Dispensation Coordinator had been called away to consult on a nicety of shipping remains to a foreign nation.

Aaron rubbed his hand across his brow and down over his sleep-deprived eyes. He leaned back in the squeaky, overstuffed chair and looked at the desk. Phia's personal possessions lay there—phone, keys, wallet. He couldn't remember ever feeling this stunned or disconnected. His mind cycled through how he might have brought Phia to Seattle two days earlier. Over and over. And over. He did not demand fairness from life but, come on, two days? Nor was he superstitious, but the rhythmic pulse in his ears made a sound of hovering, demonic wings.

"Where were we?" the coordinator asked as he returned.

"Hell if I know."

The man looked at his notes, remembered the personal items on his desk and said, "Next of kin. What is your relationship to the deceased?"

"That's tough to answer. I loved her. She loved me. She," he raised a hand to his face, "died in my lap."

The man pushed a box of tissues a fraction of an inch closer.

Aaron murmured, "She was a business partner. She

claimed me as next-of-kin on her medical forms."

The man said. "There, that is what I need. Before I let you have these items..." he gestured at Phia's stuff, "I will confirm that with the hospital."

"Can I get one thing now?"

"Sorry. There are laws."

"I need to call her aunt. Her card is in Phia's wallet. Need to see what she thinks is right."

The man dipped his head and opened his hands in commiseration, but said again, "I'm sorry."

Aaron's head dropped. "God. What's the use?"

The man paused a moment, glanced again at the items and said pointedly, "That wallet must not leave our possession until we confirm. Oh! I just remembered a thing I have to do for five minutes."

He stood and hurried from the office.

Aaron sighed, leaned his head back in the too-soft chair, and closed his raw eyes. God, he thought, why is it so complicated. Why can't they just...

His eyes snapped open and he leaned forward. He picked up the wallet, spread it open and thumbed through. There it was. He pulled the business card, closed the wallet and placed it back on the desk. Extracting his phone, he entered the aunt's contact info. Reluctantly, he stuffed the card back in Phia's wallet and laid it on the desk.

When the coordinator returned to his office, Aaron held his palm out toward him to avoid interruption.

Denise picked up her vibrating phone and looked at the caller information—nobody she knew, just a number and that number's originating state. She was going to decline but stopped. Hadn't her dying sister said something about Phia living in Idaho?

"Hello?"

Aaron said, "Is this Phia's aunt Denise?"

"Who are you?"

"Aaron Giffin. Phia's, uh, person."

No funeral. Phia's aunt agreed. What would be the point? No tree studded burial park either, but a quick cremation and permission for Aaron to do as he saw fit with the ashes.

"That poor girl," she said. "Hard enough already, but an aneurysm, too. Christ."

Aaron said, "Not much comfort, but her last day was happy."

Nick was chafing for Aaron's return, but Aaron took an extra day to drive to Westport. He parked in the seaside state park, under a clear sky with a lowering sun. He unbuckled the middle seat belt from around the canister and lifted it onto his lap. Opening the door, he swung out, stepped down, closed and locked the truck. The walk out of the lot, over the dune and down to the beach was short, but the burden of the small, grief-filled canister weighed him down to a weary trudge. For a half hour, he stood, occasionally wiping a tear from his cheek with a fingertip, gazing west as the sun crept seaward. When the sun kissed the horizon, he stepped into the water and shook Phia's ashes out on the foamy, dying waves as they fled to the sea.

end

219

www.ingramcontent.com/pod-product-compliance
Lightning Source LLC
Chambersburg PA
CBHW030330030726
47499CB00003B/717